IMAGINARY
OKLAHOMA

Tulsa, OK

WWW.THISLANDPRESS.COM

Vincent LoVoi, Publisher
Edited by Jeff Martin
Art Direction and Design by Jeremy Luther

First Edition, 2013

Printed in the United States of America

ISBN-1480036293

CONTENTS

FOREWORD

BY RIVKA GALCHEN

In Oklahoma history class as a teenager in Norman, Oklahoma, we studied the Spiro Mounds, a prehistoric Native American archaeological site whose mortuaries were looted in the 1930s. Many artifacts were ruined by grave robbers' dynamite; others were fenced to collectors; much of what remained decayed rapidly from exposure to the fresh air and so yielded few to no clues of the civilization that once was. It wasn't clear we knew that much about the Oklahoma of the present either. But at least to add to the constantly disintegrating facticity of things, there are the costumed truths of the imagination—the fertile topsoil. There are the facts of Oklahoma and then there are the facts of what that selfsame Oklahoma provokes one to imagine. Those two incomplete sets of facts together make up our best chance at some sort of binocular vision, which is still a flawed seeing of course, but one that at least lends us a depth perception superior to that of the cows.

Anyhow, the summer after graduating high school, I went on a pilgrimage along with three friends to see what we had termed the Trash Buffalo. The Trash Buffalo is a taxidermied buffalo with a vacuum inside of it that lives in the museum at the Woolaroc wildlife preserve in the Osage Hills; children search out trash throughout the surrounding park so as to set the trash before the buffalo, who then hoovers it up through his mouth; the park is therefore immaculate—that's the genius of it. At least, so it went in the story as told to us by Steve, whom we worshiped, and who was the reason we were all making the journey together, with him in tow, to see what the other three of us had never seen but took on faith. We headed out full of the hopes and dreams of the young, who, in being so at risk of boredom, can manage to make an adventure out of almost nothing.

On the long drive there was little traffic and not much scenery. The day was drizzly and overcast. We could not see far and we could have been anywhere. It was our Camino de Santiago. We passed a single sneaker on the road, as one does. Then we passed a second sneaker. Then a state trooper passed us; he U-turned across the grassy median; moments later, unseen until the last moment, he pulled us over for driving too fast, but didn't ticket us. Then we continued on our journey. Then we passed a… something. A something large and wet and smooth and brown. Was it an abandoned leather satchel? What was it a satchel of? It was, it seemed, a satchel of something very interesting. Of something quite valuable. Or illicit. Or both. But we had already passed the hastily abandoned satchel. The toll road allowed no turning back. We didn't want to get the ticket we had just not gotten. But who leaves a satchel of abandoned treasure in the middle of a wet highway? We weren't going to be those fools. We U-turned through the grassy median, then U-turned again, then pulled over on the side of the road next to the loot that would make our pilgrimage forever memorable. We got out. It was a wet brown paper bag. It fell apart when picked up.

When we got to the Trash Buffalo, it was all Steve had promised, we decided. We were also the only visitors there. That remains one of my very favorite road trips. The stories and illustrations herein are not unlike that trip. W.G. Sebald stops for in for a sandwich at an OKC café every day for a year. A constructed model whale wearing a baseball cap in Catoosa may or may not reveal something about love. Not much, we are reminded, rhymes with Tulsa. "Travelers say that all of Oklahoma is covered in a white fog," begins another of these imaginary Oklahoma tales. "The only thing visible is a tall Texaco sign, and beneath it three enormous white plastic tiles with red letters that spell out EAT." And enjoy.

RIVKA GALCHEN is a contributing editor at *Harper's*, and a member of *This Land*'s editorial advisory board. She is author of the novel *Atmospheric Disturbances*.

INTRODUCTION

BY JEFF MARTIN

"Personnel is being hired for the Theater in Oklahoma! The Great Nature Theater of Oklahoma is calling you! It's calling you today only! If you miss this opportunity, there will never be another! Anyone thinking of his future, your place is with us! All welcome! Anyone who wants to be an artist, step forward! We are the theater that has a place for everyone, everyone in his place! If you decide to join us, we congratulate you here and now! But hurry, be sure not to miss the midnight deadline! We shut down at midnight, never to reopen!"

-Franz Kafka, Amerika*

A hybrid of the visual and literary arts, *Imaginary Oklahoma* was born from a seemingly random convergence of the two. In early 2011, my wife and I visited The Modern Art Museum of Fort Worth to take in the exhibition, *Ed Ruscha: Road Tested*. Raised in Oklahoma City, Ruscha has long been a personal favorite. Known for his own melding of art and text, Ruscha's influence on this project is immense. But it wasn't the artist's body of work that lit the fuse, but rather one painting in particular. *No Man's Land* (1990), a stark commentary on his home state, planted itself in my mind instantly and remained for days after. The ghostly white outline of the pan-shaped land. The shadowy question mark stretched across the canvas, almost menacing. Like Steinbeck's "Okies," Ruscha left for California more than 30 years before the creation of this work. But it's obvious that he still wrestles

*Franz Kafka never visited Oklahoma, or America for that matter.

with Oklahoma. So do I. Anyone with an artistic bent and a progressive political persuasion would be foolish not to question his/her place here. Welcome the questions. Answer them. I grew up dying to leave, dismissing the rubes and the philistines. I can't say that I tolerate the nonsense (political, racial, anti-intellectual) any more than I used to. I probably never will. But I refuse to let them have this place. More and more, I feel a growing fellowship of the likeminded, interesting sort.

With Ruscha on the brain, casting shadows on my every thought, I picked up *The Collected Stories of Lydia Davis*, a recent (at the time) career-spanning omnibus that knocked me flat almost immediately. Known for her mastery of the super-short story, otherwise known as "flash fiction," Davis creates worlds in mere sentences. Through extreme brevity, she turns simple narrative into beautiful questions. Vague, open-ended, confusing at times, but never boring. Over the next few weeks, as Ruscha and Davis began spending more time together in my subconscious, a connection blossomed.

I began to ask my own questions. What is the place? How is it seen and regarded by that great majority in the other 49 states, and the world for that matter?

In July 2011, acclaimed writer and *New Yorker* editor Ben Greenman kicked off the series with artwork by John Lee. Nearly two years later, we now present 46 takes on the 46th state by some of the most acclaimed writers working today, each presented with a visual companion. Throughout these works, Oklahoma remains a mystery, an idea that allows the creative mind to go almost anywhere. I, for one, find this perception encouraging. Just try to imagine something interesting about Delaware.

imaginary oklahoma

ILLUSTRATION BY JOHN LEE

ALWAYS AND FOREVER

You try having a father who isn't equal to you in size. It's not easy. His boots are always bigger. His hands are always bigger. He can reach things I can't. At fifteen I find my voice is deeper than his and at first that's a victory that can't be measured, a world larger than any I can imagine. I walk around Broken Arrow telling people things they already know, just so I can be heard wielding this new instrument. But then it sinks in that it's just a voice, and that it's just a little deeper than his, and that the things it's saying are not nearly as deep. Over time the novelty drains and with it the power of the voice and I am left with the fact that when we are photographed together I look, always and forever, as if I require his protection. So you try having a father like that. And while you're at it, try having a mother who notices the difference in size, and comments on it, and even narrows her eyes when she's commenting on it as if to suggest that things could be different if only I truly wanted them different, deep down in my heart. There's an old woman in town who responds to every week of dusty summer by sitting down on the sidewalk, right there on South Main, and then looking up and announcing that she's praying for water to fall from the sky. She says she's Creek but she doesn't look it at all. Everyone accounts her a crank in more than one direction, and in the *Ledger* they have even given her a nickname: Rain Dance. But how is what my mother wants from me any better? I can look to the sky all I want and ask to be bigger but facts are facts and my father is bigger. Once I put on his shoes by accident and I was swimming in the things. Live with that at twenty, at twenty-five, at thirty. That's why I first entered a bar and why it took me years to come back out. Then one day, on the orders of the doctor, in an attempt to keep the woman I love, I came out. The sun was an affront. I visited home and my father was busy in the back but my mother fixed me a sandwich and even offered me a drink. It took all I had to refuse. Do you know what it's like to deny yourself the only thing that ever comforted you? Glass half empty? Half full? It didn't matter as long as it was beer. That was my little joke back when I made those kinds of jokes. Here's my joke now: I put on my pants one leg at a time just like any other great man. I'm so scared.

by Ben Greenman

ILLUSTRATION BY JP MORRISSON

SONGS

Oklahoma, shaped with a panhandle and a deep pan, the piece of the U.S. puzzle that I always liked to pick up early and tuck right into Texas. Oklahoma, below the Kansas of Dorothy lore and the one they wrote a song for: I bet half the residents love that musical and feel acknowledged by it and the other half resent it because the song is so damn catchy and they do not like it in their heads while the wind does its actual rushing down the plain. That same wind is a pain in the ass for crops and animals alike. That same wind drives dust into the corners of eyes and down throats. At the corner store, Sadie works at a scuffed counter selling water and snacks and beer and gas to drivers who do not want to stop there. She is not in the friendly or homey area of Oklahoma. She is in small-town transitional highway Oklahoma. She resembles the landscape with a windblown look to her skin and the pale blue eyes of certain skies in springtime. Enough already, she thinks. It is time for a new musical. It is called *Tulsa*. It does not rhyme with much of anything, but it's a mantra in her head: Tulsa, Tulsa. Full in the back of the throat, and unsentimental.

by Aimee Bender

ILLUSTRATION BY MARTIN COCCHI NAN

SEBALD SANDWICH

W.G. Sebald had a more complicated life than most readers realize. He spent the summer of 1985 in Oklahoma City, where he ate, every noon, at a modest café that I recently visited. I ordered a tongue with horseradish sauce sandwich also called, on the menu, a "Sebald sandwich." My waitress brought me an indiscriminate platter of leftover sandwiches: "I'll give you this whole tray for ten bucks," she said. I stared at the unimpressive array; I was chagrined to see that the sandwiches were on bagels, not regular bread. I told the waitress, in a tone whose uncharitableness now gives me shame to remember, "I don't want these tawdry leftovers. I want a freshly-made Sebald sandwich." From among the debris on the platter, the waitress fished out a pale approximation of a Sebald sandwich and handed it to me. I repeated my insulting demand: "I don't want an ersatz version on a skimpy bagel. I ordered a normal Sebald sandwich." After great delay, and a series of further miscommunications and disappointments, which it would be tedious to describe, I received my long-awaited Sebald sandwich. Upon finishing it, I told the harried, grumpy waitress, "Sebald was a theater person. Theater people like to eat at overpriced cafeterias. Theater people glorify these watering holes, which then become tourist attractions, like Sardi's. I distrust any restaurant that becomes a cult locale." The waitress was grumpy, but she was also talented and beautiful. She looked exactly like a young Roberta Flack, famous for "Killing Me Softly."

by Wayne Koestenbaum

ILLUSTRATION BY BEE JOHNSON

STREETLAMPS

He used to be a preacher, but now worked hanging power lines across the vast and dusty flats. Oklahoma, far from home. Towns bloomed with electric light, and in one a barefoot girl played violin by a wide brown river. Her song made him think of the Sabbath, of how he would hold children by the nose and the small of their back and lower them under the water. The girl turned to his touch, her skin the color of the water, her eyes deep. "Our world is energy unharnessed," he said, before he could stop himself. "The river's water electricity, its banks the conduit."

This was how it happened, how he'd made everyone in his life leave him. He stared out over the roiling current, wanting to switch off that thing that would not leave him. But then she touched his wrist, and her eyes smiled up at him.

"Do you like my dress?" she asked. "I made it myself."

The dress was of light tan fabric, the hem filthy with red dirt. He nodded, told her his own mother once had a dress like that. She told him her name was Purify Fox, then intently watched his face, like a challenge. He didn't know what to say and said nothing though he thought the name was beautiful. She looked away. Violin across her lap, she held her face in her hands and began to cry. She broke away and hurried off through the reeds and up the bank. He followed her into the hills, keeping his distance though he saw her glancing back over her shoulder and knew she was leading him somewhere. Soon they entered a lightless mineshaft. They walked until there was no light, and she took him by the elbow and pulled him deeper still. The darkness seemed to open, a cool breeze trickling over him. Here her violin echoed, sounding like ten, sounding like the entire world had become music. Then, in the still quiet, they stood against each other, the backs of their hands touching.

"Songs fade, but remain in the air," she whispered. "We breathe it in and it becomes a part of our skin and hair, our blood. We are a lifetime of songs. I have so many songs inside me."

He kissed her, felt, finally, somebody understood him.

At dusk, they climbed a hill high above the river, the once dark town now bright in the distance, the new row of streetlamps switching on.

by Alan Heathcock

ILLUSTRATION BY MAY YANG

THE WHALE OF CATOOSA

Washing the dishes after dinner, I couldn't stop thinking about the Whale of Catoosa, which I read about on the Internet. It's a big, not-quite-life-size, cartoonish blue whale set at the edge of a shallow body of water, as if it had come up to visit. I read that a man made the whale for his wife to commemorate the anniversary of their marriage. Then I read that this was not quite the truth. The whale was constructed sometime in the 1970s. Then, since its builder's death, the residents of Catoosa, Oklahoma have maintained it, or his family has, and it has become some kind of roadside attraction, something people stop for a few minutes to see.

It's hardly worth thinking about, but staring at a picture of the whale—it wears a little baseball cap and smiles—I think of questions: How does this whale, which could be based on a kindergartner's drawings or something weird locked deep in the inner imagination of a quiet adult, like Mount Rushmore, speak about love? How did she—the man's wife—know what it meant? What was the secret between them about whales? And is that why the citizens of Catoosa maintain it—in tribute to, if not in search of, that secret? Or is that too serious a question for such a silly and almost perverted thing?

And why did the balloon someone bought for my son's birthday last week, now only about two-thirds full of helium, venture on its own through two rooms when we weren't looking—such that I found it waiting above my daughter's changing table? Is it too much to eat an entire cantaloupe? What, finally, will result from the whale's eternal happiness? It seems to me that its smile gives something to the world while it takes something else away. Plants do this too, in a way that is helpful to humans. Are joy and irony always at war, and what happens when they strike a balance? I learn that, in fact, the whale was built by the man as part of a water slide park. Its fins are actually slides.

Could my wife have been happier? Could I? Will my daughter and son? If that balloon is a symbol, whatever it represents might not be worth understanding. And yet isn't this what it's like most days, such that the real questions can never get asked? It all goes back to the whale.

by Craig Morgan Teicher

ILLUSTRATION BY ANDREW BRINKMAN

OK, FINE

It's as if those first three lines had been wired into my brain. As if they'd always been there, since the first flutter of consciousness. The rest of the lines were extraneous. What more could one need after the rousing excess of that famous opening, followed by the later self-soothing appraisal, "You're doin' fine." Not great, not good, just fine. I always found comfort in that lack of pretension.

I sang it for days before we got in the car and once in the car I kept it up until my mother finally said, "One more time, Robbie, and you'll never see it because I'll have your father turn around and drive us straight home." The threat seemed rhetorical at best. After all, our suitcases were in the trunk and we were already halfway there. I hummed the lines under my breath, except the final "O.K." which I fixed midway between a soundless mouthing and a whisper. The lines didn't hold up under the restraint. "O.K." especially needed volume and emphasis. I stopped after three sotto voce renditions. I rolled down the window and leaned my head out. It would have sounded great out there. How loud, I wondered, would I have to shout "O.K." into the wind for it to have the necessary brio. My mother's voice was sharp, "Robbie, get your head back in. And roll that window up. Now." I slid back in the seat. I didn't take "Roll that window up" literally but more as another way of saying, "Don't do it again." I had no intention of doing it again. I formed my mouth silently around the words, exaggerating my facial expressions for drama. I kept it up until we reached the next town, which is when my father turned the car around.

by Mary Jo Bang

ILLUSTRATION BY SISHIR BOMMAKANTI

ROCK SHOP

"I'm going to move to Oklahoma," Rock Shop said, "and work in high rise construction."

We were in a bar in Little Falls, New York. Rock Shop's real name was Lawrence but his father used to own a diamond store that was called the Rock Shop and so I called him Rock Shop. By this point his father had lost the shop and then died and Rock Shop was too old to have a nickname that I'd given him in high school and I was too old to be calling him by a nickname that I'd given him in high school, but I called him Rock Shop because it was too late to start pretending he and I were something we were not, even though now Rock Shop was pretending he was going to work in high rise construction in Oklahoma and even though over the days and months and years before this we'd sat in this bar too early in the morning (it was too early in the morning) and pretended we were going to move to North Carolina, California, Florida, Georgia, and Texas and work high rise construction.

"Someone bombed Oklahoma City," he said. He'd said this earlier. This was how we'd gotten started on the subject of Oklahoma.

"How could they tell?" I said, and we laughed, even though had we looked out the window (we did not look out the window) we would have seen the building that had once been the Rock Shop and was now For Lease and had been For Lease forever and which Rock Shop and I, when we were not talking about moving somewhere warm to work in high rise construction, talked about burning to the ground for the insurance, even though neither of owned the building or its insurance policy, and even though neither of us had ever been to Oklahoma City to know what it looked like, pre- or post-bombing. We'd never been to Oklahoma. We'd never been anywhere at all.

by Brock Clarke

ILLUSTRATION BY WILLIAM GODWIN

DRINKING GAMES

KANSAS
Okay, okay, I'll go. I never had a fruit as my state vegetable.
(No one drinks.)

TEXAS
Oh, come on—are you seriously telling me you're not gonna drink for that one?

OKLAHOMA
You can look it up; my state legislature has clearly proven that a watermelon can be classified as either a fruit or vegetable. It's related to the cucumber.

TEXAS
Yeah, your state legislators are related to their cousins, more like.

OKLAHOMA
That doesn't even make sense. You know anyone who's not related to their cousins?

TEXAS
You know what I mean. Okay. I never made anybody think of a heart-warming musical. (KANSAS and OKLAHOMA both drink.)

OKLAHOMA
I never made it illegal to sell your own eye. (TEXAS drinks.)

TEXAS
I don't know why the hell not. Seems pretty sensible to me. You're up, Kansas.

KANSAS
Okay, Oklahoma: I never bragged about being a little...quick on the trigger. Sooner State. How about The Premature State? (OKLAHOMA drinks.)

OKLAHOMA
You're just jealous that no one's ever been that excited to get into Kansas.

TEXAS
I never forced bars to serve wussy low-alcohol beer. (OKLAHOMA drinks.)

OKLAHOMA
I never had a county where you couldn't buy beer at all. (KANSAS and TEXAS both drink.)

TEXAS
Yeah, okay.

KANSAS
I've never been the birthplace for a United States president. (TEXAS drinks.)

TEXAS
Of course, neither of you've seen a president die, either. That's not one I'm proud to claim.

KANSAS
True enough. (Yawns.) Well, it's getting late, and tomorrow's a workday.

TEXAS
Not for me: it's Texas Independence Day.

OKLAHOMA
Oh, yeah, I forgot how festive you are. Hey, Kansas, you want to go in with me on a San Jacinto Day card?

TEXAS
Aw, go pick on somebody your own size.

by Carolyn Parkhurst

ILLUSTRATION BY RICHIE POPE

PHAEDRA

I had always thought that roadside motels were the same anywhere in America until I wound up at a Hampden Inn off I-44 just outside Tulsa. I was en route to Santa Fe. My wife and kids had already flown out to find a house and I was driving our luggage.

My mind wanders after I've been driving for a while. So, at first, I thought I was hallucinating when I saw every chair in the motel's buffet area filled with people tuning banjos and guitars.

"What's with all this?" I asked the woman at the front desk. She had long, black hair and looked like Crystal Gayle. "Phaedra" was on her name badge.

"99 this year," she said.

"99 what?"

"Woody," she said.

Some banjo players were picking out the melody of "I Ain't Got No Home."

"Guthrie, you mean?"

"Yeah, he'd be ninety-nine this year. They're all headin' for the festival at Cain's."

"Always been more of a Lee Hazlewood man myself," I said, referencing the only Oklahoma musician that came to mind.

"Aww, me too." Phaedra's eyes ignited as if she'd found the first person who knew her language. Her voice suggested windmills, farmland, black-and-white movies, at least until she began singing "Some Velvet Morning." She had one of the loveliest voices I'd ever heard. Soon, we were trading lines—she sang the Nancy Sinatra ones; I sang the Hazlewoods.

"You should come out," she said when we were done. "I'll sing a couple."

"Coupla Lees or coupla Woodys?"

"Woody tonight," she said. "Stick around tomorrow, I might sing you a coupla Lees. You staying one night or two?"

"I'll have to see about that," I said.

My room was dank and smelled like old cigarettes, but after I cranked the AC up full, I slept until the phone rang. I looked at the clock—midnight.

"Hullo?"

"I sang my Woodys. What'd you decide? One night or two?"

"I haven't yet."

"I put you down for two. 10 PM, I get off; I'll bang on your door."

"If I'm here," I said.

"You'll be here."

Lying awake, I thought Phaedra might be right. Maybe I'd stay another night, maybe more. But my life wasn't like that Woody song they'd been playing. I wasn't ramblin' round; I had another 600 miles to travel and a family to catch up to when I was through.

I thought of saying something to Phaedra, but when I checked out, she wasn't in the lobby. I considered leaving a note, but had no idea what I'd say.

I'd been driving about four hours when my phone rang. I didn't recognize the number, but it was an Oklahoma line. I figured Phaedra was calling, but I just let the phone ring until it stopped. I had already crossed the border into Texas anyway. When I checked for a message, none was there.

by Adam Langer

PHOTO BY GERALD LANCASTER

THE PROMISE OF LABOR

One day, after Ephraim Noah had hitched up his five-year-old Fordson, climbed into the driver's seat, and bounced out over the rolling spread with the mouldboards behind him dragging lines across the field like the black type across its twice-mortgaged paper, he noticed a spark jump from one of the steel blades and something caught his eye, prompting him to idle the engine and hop down onto the sod, where he plucked from the soil a long flint knapped sharp at the edges, just the right shape to bend onto a dogwood shaft and let fly though the very air into which he gazed, cloudless and clear over the forty perfect acres everyone had wanted back in '89, until his grandfather had got to it sooner, all of it as yet untouched by oil derricks and missile silos and filled with the promise of labor, from which he had just paused, because standing there in that moment, with a suddenness that took his breath, he realized that, try as you might, pretend as you might, hope as you might, you never really own the earth.

by Stephen Dau

PHOTO BY LISA TULANE

MA BELL'S

Summer of 1976 I stayed with my cousin whose stepfather ran a restaurant called Ma Bell's in Tulsa. A telephone on every table and you called your order into the kitchen, nice gimmick at the time. The minimalist T-shirt had the name in a pleasing sans-serif, canary yellow on a blue tee. I recall the city only as sprawl, incomprehensible to my sense of urban compression. My cousin and I played golf in the horizontal blaze of a hundred-degree August afternoon, cowed after three holes. He was thirteen, I was fourteen. The next summer he visited me in New York City. I reciprocated for horizontal bafflement with the best verticality on offer. We visited the World Trade Center. Instead of taking the elevator to the tourist level at the top and paying for the view, we decided to sneak our way to the highest level we could through office corridors, to see how high a level we could attain and still get to a window for a view. I think we topped out somewhere in the eighties. It hadn't hit me until writing that last sentence that Oklahoma and Manhattan are cousins-by-terrorism. Ma Bell's is gone (broken up, I'm tempted to say) and so is his mom's marriage, and a lot of other things, but my cousin remains my cousin and he still plays golf.

by Jonathan Lethem

PHOTO BY LOGAN PIERSEN

HUNGER

The man stood at the crossroads. Cold sun cocked at noon, and he couldn't tell in what direction the roads dwindled to sky. The fields were corn but so drought-struck the plants were miniature. He didn't know how he got there, where he was going.

Something about his wife, maybe. Lilian? he tried to call, but his throat was dry, and he could only rasp.

He took a foot from one slipper and looked at it. It was bloody, one toenail ripped off. He thought he had probably been walking a long time. It was pleasant to stand. The sunlight warmed his shoulders and the wind blowing through his clothes wasn't so cold.

When he looked up again, the sun had just gone down. It was twilight now.

On one of the roads, a speck was growing. He saw first that it was red, then that it was a pickup. And now there was sound, a wash of engine and some kind of thumping music. The truck slowed and stopped.

There were two boys looking at him. Hair sun-blond, noses freckled. Waft of bourbon. On the seat between them sat a toy bat, rubber on the outside and an aluminum core.

Hey, old man, the driver said, and the other boy flicked off the music. What're you doing all the way out here?

The old man cleared his throat and said, Wife.

She left you here? said the boy in the passenger seat.

Like an old dog, said the driver out of the corner of his mouth. Tired of his stink. The boys laughed. And now the old man could smell himself, terrible, sweat and piss and his own loose bowels. He felt ashamed.

Lilian? he whispered.

Darkness fell on the road. The driver flicked on the lights and the old man blinked. He seemed even frailer, illuminated so.

The driver said, Let's have some fun, and reached for the bat and the handle of his door.

But his friend had seen the tag on the man's wrist and recognized it from visiting his own grandfather. He said, Nah. Not worth it. Let's get waffles.

The driver put the truck in gear and they moved off. The boy in the passenger seat turned on the music again and watched in the rearview as the old man became a blot on the darkness, then a distant moonlit point. Dementia, poor soul. At the Dairy Palace, he went to the bathroom and called his uncle, the sheriff, about the escapee, then, duty done, put him from his mind.

But something clung to him, an echo under his conscious thoughts. And, at the soggy end of winter, when his girlfriend broke up with him for a boy in Chicago she'd met online, the heartbreak whipped itself into a terrible energy. He packed his bags in the darkness and left a note for his mother. Kissed his sleeping brother. At dawn he took off, in no particular direction, toward something urgent, something unknown.

by Lauren Groff

PHOTO BY RICHARD ORTEGA

THE TIGERS OF THE OKLAHOMA POOL HALLS, A TAXIDERMILOGICAL REPORT

TUPELO TAXIDERMY, TUPELO, OK, 74572
TUEPLO HASSMAN, PROPRIETOR

Referring to the past, "back in the day," we moved through the jungle late at night. The night is a jungle, usually habituated by tigers. Our undergarments were stained with fear of tigers, eyes of tigers in our drawers that blinked as we ran, far from each other, constellated as pool balls after a hard break, hips slammed to table, solids separate from stripes. We mistook each other for tigers. Eventually we had our undergarments off, completely naked, as is usually done in protest of tigers. We raised diamond yellow flags, and paraded through the jungle of baize, the stacks of quarters on the pool table shaking with each stomp of our feet as we protested the tigers that stalked us and the tigers we feared we'd become.

We walked late at night, from one jungle to the next; led by someone's older brother who had given up his pants years before. We all thought we'd give up our pants soon enough. The diamond yellow pattern of fear attracts tigers, is mistaken for a strange tiger's wink in the dark by territorial tiger eyes. In this way, patterns encroach upon and destroy themselves. In this way, tufts of fur and bits of elastic band scatter in the wind. We lost many friends on our way home from the pool hall. Some were eaten by tigers. Some turned into adults. In a state shaped like a gun you must choose between the barrel and the chamber. When you live inside a hatchet you are the handle or the blade.

by Tupelo Hassman

LANCASTER

REST STOP

The woman was angry when she got to Ray's register, and Ray was already thinking of all the things that weren't his fault: the food, the traffic, how the McDonald's sat in the turnpike service island like a pimple, flat-faced Oklahoma stretching clear-skinned around it. She held her daughter's hand, the girl so small and uncurious she didn't bother to look up at Ray, just held her eyes smack ahead into the edge of the counter.

"The bathrooms are roped off," the mother said.

"I'm sorry. Plumbing issue." Don't get into details with the guests, Ray's supervisor had told him. Just keep it closed till a crew gets there.

"They're closed at the gas station, too," she said, which Ray's supervisor hadn't mentioned. "My little girl needs to go."

Ray shrugged, even though he knew it would just piss the woman off, the way it pissed off Susanna every time she asked what he wanted for dinner, what movie to see, whether it was worth driving the thirty minutes to a theater at all. He meant them, the shrugs, honest appraisals of his own uncertainty. He didn't know what this woman should do, any more than he knew what to tell Susanna about her plan: the cousin in Arizona, the place to crash while they looked for work. He just didn't know, and pretending like he did seemed to add more bullshit to the already fragrant world.

"The next service area's forty miles from here," the woman prodded, and Ray nodded sympathetically. The turnpike had been built miles from everything, the towns hidden to the north and south. A driver could cross half the state without seeing a sign of human habitation. Ray thought about telling the woman to take the exit—his town was just four miles away. There was a café on the main drag still, with bad coffee but decent burgers. Susanna would steer them straight, tell them what to order. He could tell the woman to tell Susanna that Ray sent his love.

"What good is that?" Ray imagined Susanna asking. "You send me love and a shitty tipper. That's not what this place needs." Ray wondered what exactly their place did need. How could you lure travelers off the road when they couldn't see what was waiting for them? Last summer he and Susanna had taken a road trip. In southern Arizona there were 300 miles of signs for The Thing. *THE THING? WHAT IS IT*? the billboards shrieked, as if the owner himself weren't sure.

"It's just a mummy," Susanna had said, looking it up with some trucker's smart phone when they stopped for gas. When they passed the exit, she wouldn't let Ray stop. "You've got no sense of mystery," Ray had said, when what he really meant was no sense of loyalty, no feeling for the Thing ticket takers, the Thing postcard sellers, all those souls clinging to the highway.

"I'm no sucker," Susanna had said, and Ray shrugged.

"You unlock it or I take her out behind your dumpster," the woman said. "The girl's gotta go."

Ray thought about his town. He thought about Susanna. What could keep people anywhere when all they really wanted was to keep moving?

Ray shrugged and reached under the counter for a bathroom key. "If the girl's gotta go, she's gotta go."

by Caitlin Horrocks

PHOTO BY SHANE BROWN

OKLAHOMA IS FOR LOVERS

Nobody in the office knows for sure if fat, ugly Larry Leibovitch really did see this coming. To hear him tell it, Larry was prescient—claims to have noticed the pattern years ago. A raft of celebrity divorces here. Dropping enrollment there. Shitty TV shows getting canceled due to a dwindling supply of brides to humiliate. And a new girlfriend, Larry's first, inexplicably willing and eager to kiss his fat face. "I knew right then that something strange was going on," he once told an interviewer from the *Hugo Daily*. "It wasn't just out there. What they lost … we were getting it."

Most of us suspect it was just a combination of luck and laziness. Three years ago, when Larry slapped "Oklahoma is for Lovers" on the banner of the TravelOK website, it wasn't nothing but a headache. Jackasses from the Virginia Tourism Authority were ceasing and desisting us by the end of the day. Much as we wished Larry'd shown a little more creativity in his sloganeering, we didn't like being told what to do, so we decided to fight it. But in the time it took to get to a judge, the world changed. Larry's slogan became manifestly true.

Everywhere but here, people fell hard out of love. Babies and weddings and awkward first dates straight up stopped happening. By the time the President got kicked out—we watched him live on the south lawn, the former first lady on the balcony hurling down suits and wingtips and heavy ethnic bric-a-brac shed by visiting dignitaries—it could hardly be called a watershed moment. "I told you," Larry said the following day, as he passed out his wedding invitations. "What did I tell you?"

No one knows why or how it happened—like God himself pulled a plug somewhere near Tulsa, all that love flowing inward like spring melt. Blessed as we are with this bounty, it's hard to not feel sorry for anybody who doesn't live here. It's hard to see their betrayed, empty, forlorn faces on TV. And even though we caught the winning end of this deal, we all wish things would go back to the way they were. Even those of us with the most to lose, like fat, ugly Larry Leibovitch. He loves everybody enough to know that nobody deserves this.

by Alexander Yates

PHOTO BY ROSIE LOVOI

DRIVER'S ED

The girl had been slumping behind the driver's seat, pleading silently for her own death, when the mountain lion struck, its great gray paws putting a sizable dent in the center of the vehicle's beige hood; the girl had just taken a right-hand turn down Snow Road, and had forgotten to signal first, and Mr. Flutie, the driver's education instructor—with his brambly red beard, feverishly hairy knuckles, and drab plaid shirt—had taken notice, shaking his head, jabbing angrily with his pen at the clipboard tilted upon his chest; Marissa—the girl, aged sixteen, had been late in getting her license because she had been rigorously homeschooled, and the thought of her roaming the unpatrolled roads alone, without a guardian or chaperone, had weighed heavily upon her parents' hearts until a weekend job had opened up for the girl at Lawton's only Christian roller-skating rink *Holy Rollers*—Marissa now saw the beast staring at her confusedly through the automobile's windshield and forget her brief training, turning the wheel to the furthest right, running the car up the curb directly into an unpainted mailbox-post; the sleek-muscled animal then bounded off the hood, slipping through the stalled traffic in a single, inelegant bounce; while in the backseat, Jeremiah—also sixteen, face rendered unlovable by the depredations of acne, having also been wistfully dreaming of his own death, having also been forcibly schooled at home—let out an audible cry of shock. Afterwards, while waiting for the tow truck, while waiting for Mr. Flutie to stop hyperventilating, while waiting for their unhappy families to come pick them up, Jeremiah leaned over and took in the smell of Marissa's gloriously blonde hair. For the boy, the sight of the cougar staring at him through the front windshield of the car became as prismatic, as unknowable as the previously considered face of God.

by Joe Meno

ILLUSTRATION BY JANE RADSTROM

TOM MIX

1968, and we are going to the Museum of Tom Mix. It is in a place called Dewey. "Dewy" is what my father calls my sister. A dewy girl. She lowers her eyes to not see him looking at her. I have my guns on, I buckle them on every morning when I put on my jeans. They have ivory handles with rearing horses carved on them that look like Tony, Tom Mix's horse. My father's name is Tony too. There is a horse on the hood of the car, and my father said we follow that horse wherever it goes. I watched for the horse to turn right or left, to see if the car went that way, and every time it did. But I am older now and I get it. Tony was a trick pony. My mother says that my father is a one-trick pony. Tony can think and talk almost like a person (Tony the horse). The Museum of Tom Mix is Tom Mix, but Tom Mix is much larger than you would think, taller than the statue of Paul Bunyan in that other town. We go around to the back of his left boot, which has a heel as high as I am, with a door in it. We go in one by one. There is a stairway up to the top of Tom Mix, and it is dark at the top. Tony is there, halfway up; then above Tony is the other Tony, after Tony died, and above him another. Far, far up are Tom Mix's narrowed eyes, letting in the light. We are standing together, I love them all, and we wait to see who will start to climb.

by John Crowley

ILLUSTRATION BY SHANE MCDERMOTT

WAILING WALL

She prays for world peace. Then she leans her head against the stone and cries. Because when given her moment in Jerusalem, when faced with holiness, that was what she came up with. Her prayers were the prayers of beauty pageant contestants.

What she really wants to ask for is a Coke, because she's thirsty, and help for her brother, because he drinks too much, and a safe flight home, because airplanes scare her. What she really wants is to see that guy again, the one she'd met in a bar in Tel Aviv. He was from Oklahoma, and so tall that to see him, she'd leaned back on her heels and lifted her eyes. She lost her balance but he caught her, one arm around her waist. *There are Jews in Oklahoma?* she said, and they both laughed. Then she leaned her head on his chest.

Now the stone is rough against her palms and forehead, and it's warm—from the sun maybe, or the hands pressed against it on both sides. Anyone would think she was grieving. But she cries because she's a tourist, like everyone else. She cries because nearby people are dying, back home her brother is dying, and here she is, thirsty. She cries because she once believed—in God, yes, but also in her right to speak to Him, her ability to interest Him. She cries because she'll never see that boy from Oklahoma again. She cries because she can't remember his name. She cries because to the left of her, and to the right, everyone else is crying too.

by Deborah Willis

PHOTO BY LAZLOW JONES

THE FAN

It's all too easy for a fan to become overwhelmed by the volume of Grateful Dead music that is and continues to be made available by Grateful Dead Productions and so I have invented a system that I use to impose self-discipline on my consumption of Grateful Dead music and maybe this system can be useful for you, too. What I do is I peg my buying (of concerts, box sets, or other live compilations) to certain key dates throughout the year: my birthday, Jerry Garcia's birthday, the anniversary of Jerry's death, for Christmas, and also any time I'm looking at a show on Dead.net and see that the date of the show and today's date are the same. That's the wild card that makes the system fun, and it was in this way that I first came to own 5/2/70 (*Dick's Picks #8,* Binghamton, NY), 12/16/92 (*Dick's Picks #27*, Oakland, CA), 6/18/76 (*Grateful Dead Download Series Vol. 4,* Passaic, NJ) and *Dick's Picks #30*: highlights from 3/25, 27, 28/72 at the New York Academy of Music, which I actually bought on a 3/26 so it technically broke the rules but I figure, Hey, the Grateful Dead were all about breaking the rules!

Right after the Academy shows the Dead went on their first tour of Europe, and played the shows that would be culled for such releases as *Europe '72, Hundred Year Hall, Steppin' Out with the Grateful Dead: England '72*, and *Rockin' the Rhein with the Grateful Dead.* People say that Europe '72 was the best Grateful Dead tour ever but I think that they are overlooking Fall 1973—an American tour—which is woefully under-mythologized if, admittedly, pretty well-documented. Fall '73 began in Oklahoma City, Oklahoma on 10/19 (aka *Dick's Picks #19*) and ended two months later on 12/19 in Tampa, Florida (*Dick's Picks #1*). Other Fall '73 releases include *Dick's Picks #14* (11/30 and 12/2, Boston, MA), *Road Trips Vol. 4 No. 3* (11/21 at the Denver Coliseum with filler from 11/20 at the same venue), *Grateful Dead Download Series Vol. 8* (12/10 in Charlotte, NC) and *Winterland 1973: The Complete Recordings,* a nine-disc box set of the full concerts from 11/9, 10 and 11/73 at Bill Graham's Winterland Ballroom in San Francisco. (This box set should not be confused with *Winterland June 1977: The Complete Recordings,* which has similar artwork and is also nine discs).

Though I must admit that I have not yet purchased—indeed have never heard so much as a note from—10/19/73 it feels as if this show, being the opening night of Fall '73, is fundamentally already part of my life. It is as if the very word "Oklahoma" whispers to me "fifteen and a half minute 'Dark Star' segues into ten and a half minute 'Mind Left Body Jam.'" I'm familiar with the set list, obviously, so even though my system has yet to yield it up to me it is really just a matter of "All good things in all good time," as Jerry says—on one of his solo records, but still.

My two favorite things about *Winterland 1973* are (1) the mind-blowing musical palindrome of "Playin'>UJB>AM Dew>UJB>Playin'" that opens set two on 11/10, and (2) the fact that it put Fall '73 over the top in terms of extensiveness of documentation relative to Europe '72. Or it did until this year, because now they're releasing a sixty-one-disc box set which will present the Europe '72 tour in its entirety. Every note of all twenty-two shows. It's really not fair, because how can you ever top everything? Though of course maybe the band or the company that now manages their catalog doesn't see it as a competition. There are, by one estimate I saw on a tee shirt, 2317 Grateful Dead shows comprising 417,600 hours of music performed over the course of thirty years. Maybe one day they will release it all. The whole archive out there and each show like a brick in the great Grateful Dead pyramid (speaking of which: the Grateful Dead actually played at the pyramids in Egypt in 1978). I don't know if that'll ever happen, but it definitely should and seems like it probably will. In the meantime I can tell you this: if they ever do make a *Fall 1973: The Complete Recordings* it will have twenty-seven shows and fill seventy discs with a half hour left over on the seventy-first disc for filler. The thing about the filler is you don't want to treat it like an afterthought. You want to make the most of the space available and pick the best songs you can. I have some ideas about this too, of course, but I don't want to get ahead of myself.

by Justin Taylor

PHOTO BY RICHARD ORTEGA

ARBUCKLE RIFT

In Ponca City, the left tendon, being the more rational, was ready to turn back for Roanoke. It hadn't wanted to stray in the first place, but out of a long-standing loyalty, it conceded to the right tendon's request to continue south.

Omar couldn't name this restlessness. His letters to Roanoke gave wide berth to the issue of his absence and focused instead on the mare he'd chosen. How she could read the delicate contractions and buffeted strikes of his calf muscles was beyond Omar; he'd barely ridden before. He gave little thought to the allograph transplant he'd undergone as a young boy—two Achilles tendons taken from a cadaver to replace his damaged set. The donor had also been a young boy, a descendant of the Chickasaw Indian Nation struck dead by a train.

When Omar reached Robber's Roost in the Arbuckle Mountains the tendons took in vistas of trembling prairie grass, grazing bison and the Rock Creek corridor winding its way south through the Platt. "I'm delighted," the right tendon said. "After so many concessions, Indian Territory."

"If you can't beat 'em, join 'em," the left tendon grumbled. "I say we go back."

"It appears we're at a crossroads," the right said frostily.

Omar stood then, stretched his legs. It was beautiful country. The horse waited in a patch of scouring rush, turning its jaw like a delicate rock tumbler.

"Let Omar decide," the left suggested.

"It's his life," the right acceded. "Although this land's the very last of us."

But Omar's gaze had already risen above the Platt, ventured south beyond the Lake of the Arbuckles, alighted on what he imagined were the forks and spools of the river that kept him from Texas.

by Nancy Mauro

PHOTO BY LISA TULANE

RIGHT BEHIND THE RAIN

Let me explain something: Oklahoma was not my idea.

It happened this way. We were having hamburgers at Sonny's Grill in Soho, on Chater Street, four of us from work, all except Feng, who insists on eating spaghetti bolognese whenever we go out for Western food. Spaghetti bolognese, which, fortunately, every non-Chinese restaurant has in Hong Kong, except McDonald's. What do you do at McDonald's, I asked him, and he said, I never go to McDonald's. The whole place always stinks of cheese.

He has a pathological fear of cheese. Makes the waitress swear that the bolognese has no cheese in it, or on it, and waves away the little bowl of parmesan anxiously, as if it's plutonium. He hates cheese the way Swedes hate MSG.

I should say that we're a little United Nations in our office, not that there's anything so unusual about it these days. Brits, Malays, Taiwanese, French, Mainlanders, and Queenie, our secretary, the one lonely local girl. But no Americans. Americans, Nathan says, can't invent brands. They are brands. It's like asking an elephant to be a zoologist.

Nathan is from New Zealand, started out as a Barry Manilow impersonator in Tokyo, but made his fortune in a string of backpacker bars in Pattaya. His book, *This Is Not My Life: Adventures of a Brand Consultant,* is a bestseller in Hyderabad.

So in this case the company is from Xiamen. Big deal, you say, another denim plant in Xiamen. But no, there's serious money behind this one. Same money that came up with the Nikes that even the Nike CEO couldn't tell weren't real. And some kind of designer from San Francisco, a jeans guru, who happens to be originally Fujianese. A little ethnic solidarity happening up there. They've got all these patterns—Abercrombie, Hollister, Levis. Don't ask me how it happens. And they want a complete turnaround, the whole package, mock-ups, billboards, models, everything, in ten days. So: Oklahoma.

Yvan was the first one to say the word. He had a pocket-sized atlas he'd picked up at Page One, a French atlas, and he was reading out all these place names in a horrible Serge Gainsbourg voice, so that they reminded you of Gauloises and incest. Toh-pee-kaaah. Deh Mwahn. Dahnver. Ohh... kalahohmaah.

Try saying it in Chinese, Janice said. She's from Newcastle, a skeptic. But no, Feng said, that's the point. We can't pronounce Bain de Soleil either. We can't pronounce Bordeaux.

It sounded so—chewy. That's what I liked about it. All those round vowels and one crazy dipthong. Kla. It sounded like someone yelling something over a great distance. Hey, Francis said, staring at his phone, it turns out there's a famous opera about it. And he played a little of one of the songs over his tinny speaker. I recognized it from my Miles Davis records. "If I Were A Bell." So, I thought, that's Oklahoma.

•••

It wasn't long after the big release, the fashion show, the carbide lamps, the pulsing bottles of cheap San Andreas Valley champagne, that I started having the nightmares. I was in a cornfield being kicked by elephants. I was pursued down a dirt road by naked men on motorcycles. Someone kept talking about being raped by the wind. I came down with a nasty flu, and all I could think about, in all those hours of heaving over the tiles, was cheese. Cheese melted over salads, cheese poured onto ice. French fries coated in chocolate and dipped in cheese.

That was all I could think of, when I ventured back out onto the streets, and saw the word stitched across a thousand curving rear ends. Elephants and cornfields and rivers of cheese.

I had another nightmare just last night in which all my money, every bill, every credit card, every bank statement, was made of corn. You could eat it.

The problem with a name is that you can't unsay it. I live in Oklahoma now. The fields have closed in around me, and I can't go back.

by Jess Row

PHOTO BY JOHN DEMMING

DOLL

In the old shed, behind the old chicken house, across the old garden which had grown nothing but sawgrass for years, Clara found the girl sawing the left leg off the old doll. The doll had been Clara's mother's, old but well-preserved, her painted eyes still a startling blue.

Clara had heard the sawing from the house. Now she heard that the girl was humming, too, a song her mother hummed as she mopped Clara's floors.

The humming stopped when the girl noticed Clara. Lucia was her name. She was only nine or ten but she looked at everything as if she'd seen it before. She set down the saw and waited.

Even the saw was old. It had belonged to Clara's brother, who lived in Phoenix now with another man and a whirlpool. The others had gone east. There was only Clara left, and her husband, whose job at the U was too good to give up.

The girl waited. Clara had blamed her mother, Carmen, for the doll's disappearance. She had accused her then not fired her. She felt sorry for Carmen, and she was used to her, and the other women who cleaned were full-blooded Mexicans whereas Carmen was known to have some Creek in her. Clara had been raised with the idea that Indians were drunk but kind—susceptible—whereas Mexicans, rarer in those days, were drunk and mean.

Clara would have to apologize to Carmen. She would have to tell her not to bring the girl anymore. The girl made Clara nervous anyway, surprising her from corners, just sitting there staring back, her brown eyes refusing to be sorry or afraid.

Clara grabbed the doll, but the girl let go so easily she tripped backward—Clara's shoulder hit the shed's doorframe and the dead weight of the doll repulsed her suddenly, the painted arm in her hand a stiff, shabby shell. She took the thing by the hair instead, turned, and left, and Lucia, who knew that the woman had tried to have babies, whose mother had stayed working for her only because she pitied her this trying, kept her eyes on the woman's back, which began to shake, and on her ankles, which turned in the divots between the old garden rows.

by Anna Solomon

PHOTO BY ELIJAH ANDERSON

THE OKLAHOMA PORTLAND CEMENT COMPANY

Despite taking its name from the first postmaster's daughter, Ada earned a reputation as one of the roughest cattle towns in the Southwest. Gun slinging, cattle rustling, frontier justice, Ada withstood 36 murders in 1909, as well as threats of range war between the area's two largest ranches, one run by former U.S. Marshall Gus Bobbit, the other by Joe Allen and Jesse West.

Early April 1909, as Bobbit and a ranch hand drove two wagons into town, a hired killer shot the men dead with a shotgun. After years of corrupt officials, bribes, unpunished murders, Adans took the law into their own hands and started a manhunt for James Miller, a cool killer with more than 30 deaths to his credit. They caught him in Texas, brought him back, and at 2:30 in the morning, sheriff and deputies conveniently absent, vigilantes took the prisoner to an old livery barn. Before the inevitable, there was a hushed pause as the crowd tried to get Miller to talk about the murder. "Come on, come on," he said to the crowd, "let's get this over with as soon as possible."

The busy undertaker who cared for these dead was A.L. Mossman. In the window of his mortuary shop, Mossman displayed his equally rememberable passion: rock collecting. The reputation of his geological specimens spread as far as Indiana, and Adam Beck ventured west to peruse Mossman's stones. The mortician led the industrialist on a prospecting survey of Pontotoc County, in the Chickasaw Nation. After the tour, Beck decided to locate a cement plant in the rich limestone region and purchased a quarry just outside Ada.

Thus, Beck organized and founded the Oklahoma Portland Cement Company. The original, dry-process plant consisted of two kilns, 125 feet long, with a daily capacity of 1,000 barrels. On Christmas Day 1907, little more than a month after statehood, almost two years before the infamous hanging, the Ada plant burned its first clinker. Cement soon shipped out by train, in large wooden barrels, to Texas and points east.

by William Lychack

PHOTO BY JOHN DEMMING

FIND YOUR OKLAHOMA

"I once knew a man from a town in Texas," he said to us, "small but not hickville, there was a college there, where he taught. Taught classes on weekdays and on weekends played a hanky-panky with his wife," he said, "that involved pretending she was an amputee. She would strap her lower leg up behind her thigh, with his assistance, and go around in a knee-length skirt and crutches, hopping on the one serviceable leg. People assumed she had lost the other one in a terrible accident of some kind. The two of them were well known in the town where they lived, which bordered Oklahoma, too well known to go around town as if the wife were believably an amputee, so they went across stateliness. They would dip into Oklahoma for 'erotic weekends,' in places where no one knew them. That was an important thing, that they go where no one knew them. They would head north to Lawton, or Oklahoma City, once to Enid, which was the woman's name, and another time to Slaughterville, which the man found humorous and Enid did not. They would arrive in Slaughterville or Enid in their respective play-act roles, a stoic amputee crutching her way into a motel office with the help of her doting caretaker. They would check into their room and then go to a restaurant, where they received looks of shy condolence from the hostess and waiters and the other clientele, order as if they were on some kind of significant date, an anniversary, say, in these special occasion restaurants where the waiter comes to the table with a pepper grinder that's five feet tall. You know what I mean. Heavy and oversized furniture, ugly American-colonial lighting, either too bright or too dark, places where the wine is some kind of grapey burgundy served in a carafe by pimply waiters in bowties, small town goobers trained by the management to congratulate you on your order. Excellent choice, sir. Since having selected from their clichéd and obvious menu is proof of your inherent cleverness. As they ate their chops and drank their burgundy and took in the shabby ambiance, the husband covertly fondled his wife's stump under the table, her not-real stump, her play-stump. The two or even three carafes of burgundy staining in, blurring inhibitions, they would return to the motel. The man, drunk now, and good and ready to get into the real business, would remain ever-patient and solicitous with his handicapped wife, helping her out of the car and to the room, carrying her over the threshold like a child bride being airlifted into a territory of freshness and anticipation, the lightness of his wife's body in the man's arms somehow exactly the weight of her light compliance. He would set her softly on the bed. Proceed to undress her slowly, with meaningful pauses and great care. Eye contact, deep and even breathing. Extra attention to her knee-stump, the surface of it, rounded but with shallow areas, like a very smooth rock, the knee. And then touching the cold bed below the knee, the emptiness of it. A complicated thrill, which I myself can only imagine. 'Not for the layperson' was what this man said of their game, an advanced level of fantasy and humping. The idea of her missing leg was a shared space between them, it was practically a religion and they didn't want to give it up.

"At the end of these Oklahoma weekends," he said, "when for the return home she released her hidden leg, unstrapped it so that her 'stump' was yet again just a normal healthy knee, the sight of it there in front of her was beyond painful for both of them. The real leg contradicted everything. It ground the memories of their romantic weekends to nothing. The wife, her two healthy legs stretched out, would sob inconsolably all the way home. This distressed her husband, as you can imagine. And he had his own interest in hoping to find a solution to their problem. So they began to inquire. They saw various doctors at various clinics. Nobody was interested in helping them. One or two medical professionals even threatened to call the police, suggesting that the man could be arrested. Which is another topic for another discourse. But briefly, why is the common good dependent upon preventing these two semi-free individuals from removing something that belongs to them, and that they both agree must be disposed of? What interest do we have in her leg that she herself does not have? Because I must confess I am among those who would want it to stay attached to the rest of her, even as this seems an abuse of governance, and an imposition on the victimless sexual satisfaction of two people, as I said, semi-free. Last time I talked to this man, we have lost touch, the reason for which you'll learn in a moment, anyhow the last time I heard from him, he and his wife had finally found some kind of doctor down in the Yucatan who was willing to perform the operation, and apparently there was a community there, for rehabilitation and general lifestyle support. They were planning to relocate from XX, and to make their Oklahoma weekends something permanent and irreversible. The man wrote to me and said, *Our dream will soon be coming true. We've found our Oklahoma, down in Quintana Roo.*"

"And here I arrive at my point," he said to us.

What was his point?

"The point is that everyone has a different dream. The point is that it is a grave mistake to assume your dream is shared, that it's a common dream. Not only is it not shared, not common, there is no reason to assume your dream is not actively hated by other people. That they don't find you and it disgusting. Always go to another state, an Oklahoma so-called, if you want to live your dream without judgment."

by Rachel Kushner

ILLUSTRATION BY AMAYA MASON

SHOWBIZ FOLK HERO

With four hysterical little girls running from my left and from my right, I could only think of one thing: I never wanted to go to Oklahoma.

A month earlier, when my dance teacher announced that the whole school, including my intermediate tap class, was going to entertain Evening Star Retirement Village in a Broadway-themed show because old people would already know the words to the songs, I was pretty excited. I was 12. It would be my first real performance for people I wasn't related to and I was eager to show off my showbiz skills, of which I assured myself I had many. I was dedicated. I could sing just like Judy Garland if the music was loud enough. I had a bold ball change.

While other classes danced to "The Sound of Music" and snapped along to "West Side Story," we shuffled off to "Oklahoma!" as the audience of the infirmed, dazed, and the mummified barely gazed in our direction as tiny, pin-sized beads of sweat formed a horizon over my upper lip. I hit every mark and was in time to the music, even as the four-year old next to me spun out of control and unprofessionally wandered the "stage," which was really just a cleared-out space at the end of the cafeteria.

It didn't matter. I was in it for the reward, the shower of applause that our audience was about to deliver after the chorus ended and we finished big with a heel click, turn, and jazz hands.

But that didn't happen. Instead, from the back of the cafeteria, an old man, his face sagging and folded, rolled himself to the front of the "stage."

"We know we belong to the land/
And the land we belong to is grand ..."

And at first, I wasn't sure what was happening. Sure, I was 12, but I had two sisters, no brothers. And we were Roman Catholic. Biology hid behind a dark curtain in our house. In a box that was hammered shut with nails of shame.

"And when we say /
Yeeow! Ayipioeeay!"

The things I was sure of were this: The old man's fly was open, I know because I watched him unzip it. And suddenly, a puddle began to spread on the floor, bigger, larger, heading right toward a big finish, as was I.

Not even the shrieks of my fellow cast could divert my attention. If you're showbiz folk, you're showbiz folk. Everybody else should just buy a ticket. I had a routine to finish, and I was there to entertain my audience. Even the one who was getting pulled away from the stage and now had paper napkins stacked in his lap by a nurse. I was a dancer, I was going to dance until I was the only one on stage as the other performers shot off stage with looks of horror and the unprofessional four-year old was hyperventilating. My teacher lifted the needle off the record player and the only sound that could be heard in the cafeteria was the lone tap-tap-tap of me forging on with my unplanned solo.

It was definitely not, in any way, OK.

by Laurie Notaro

PHOTO BY ROSIE LOVOI

LINGUISTICS

I learned how to identify an Oklahoma accent on a date. My mom's from Corpus. It's a subtle difference, but you can definitely tell. I was anxious. It wasn't the guy, it was a bad time, my entire twenties. I wasn't on venlafaxine and benzos yet. People talk about being in a drug haze. I was in a haze from a lack of drugs. Not a haze—hyperkinesis, agita, bad judgments. It was summer in D.C., hot and humid. I can't remember the guy's name. I think we'd met at JR's. He was handsome like Steve McQueen. He was shorter than me, maybe 5'8" and with a lanky build. I'm 6'1". He had gray hair at twenty-whatever. I couldn't believe how normal and masculine he was. It was so what I was looking for, but bipolar II took away, among other things, my ability to manage my own mind. We must have gone to dinner, in the Dupont Circle area, it's where we all clustered then. It was 1988 and Clinton hadn't been elected yet. I was living there because by coincidence my grad school was on Mass Ave and 17th. Japanese political economy. Nihon no seiji-gaku. $20k a year.

I have this image of us walking on Connecticut Avenue. He was easy-going. I focused on his accent. I'm great at reproducing accents.

He invited me back, or else we sort of drifted back to his place. It was still light out. He had the air blasting. We did a little of that yes-no-maybe dance but got to making out pretty fast. Anything I wanted in those days, I somehow screwed it up. I'd gotten him down to just his jeans. He'd been drinking a Coors. His frame felt even slighter now my hands were on him, but he felt strong. He grinned. "You wanna try and take me?" The Oklahoman accent is very slightly looser than Dallas and palpably slower.

"Try" is a manly bet and a provocation both. "Take me," a formulation antiquated since the late 19th century, erudite and elegant as hell.

I think I didn't do it. I think it was too much. I just don't remember. How can you remember some things so clearly and not others? I think that's how it worked, the disease just leached away from you everything that was good, everything you would have loved and, being able to love it, been happy.

by Chandler Burr

ILLUSTRATION BY MICHELLE DUCKWORTH

STILLWATER

The boy at the bottom of the lake opened his eyes and found his right hand had floated free again despite his efforts. His legs and torso were partially wedged under an enormous tree trunk and he watched the free hand, slightly luminescent, casting a glow like moonlight. The grit and sediment in the water burned his eyes as he squinted in the gloom, discerning the surface far above him as mirror of dark glass. His hip and shoulder ached from the weight of the tree, but the right side of his body still urged him toward the surface. He waited another hour then gave up, allowing his body to slide out and ascend slowly into starlight.

Someone walking the woods along the southern edge of the lake on that November night might have seen him emerging from the water, his forehead breaking the smooth black surface of the quiet lake and the slow plod of his steps as he waded to shore among the cattails and jimson weed. They might have seen him stand on the bank, shivering, watching the waters of the lake reverberate with his departure and then come to complete stillness again. Wind pulled at the tops of the shadowy forest, the supple trunks of the trees wending, and when he listened the air was full of windfall and bird alarm. The boy crept into the woods and curled at the base of a thick pine, pulling a heavy mat of needles over him like a blanket and prepared to weather the long night that seemed like it would never end.

At daybreak the boy was already moving, working his way back through to the hard road that led into town. His clothes were still damp and he chuffed and gasped with the cold as he kept to the treeline, ducking away from cars, until he made the gas station with the outside bathroom. He locked the door and took off his clothes and dried them the best he could with paper towels, wiping away mud and lake debris. He used his fingers to comb his hair, making a rudimentary part to one side. In the dirty mirror his dough-like face warped and vibrated and the boy shut his eyes.

Later he stood in the playground by the fence, warily watching the other children and parents. He was too old for this place, but it was the best he could do. The people of the town became used to the sight of this slightly disheveled boy, lurking on the perimeter, but no one made a move to befriend him and parents called out angrily for their children when they ventured in his direction.

It was a different time. In those days a boy could exist on the edge for a long while before anyone thought to inquire about him or offer assistance. The woods were said to be filled with such boys, scrawny, dirty-necked youths who filtered through backyard floodlights and crouched behind the woodpile. Stories were told of boys floating on the surface of the lake, hundreds of them, face up to the moon, their large eyes unblinking. But there really was only the one boy, the one who has been here in Stillwater forever, the boy we see here now, leaning on the chain link fence, watching our beautiful children playing in the sandbox, building their tiny imaginary universes.

by Matt Bondurant

ILLUSTRATION BY JOHN LEE

RICH RICE FROM TULSA

Carl's roommate, Rich Rice, had gone home to Tulsa for spring break. There were six of us in Carl's room, with jobs or low funds or sex plans, staying on campus, trying not to think of *The Shining* as we walked home each night past abandoned white message boards, past forgotten laundry. There was no TV. No one cared about the party we'd been invited to by the drunk townie at the Harris Teeter.

Jen, Laing's girlfriend, rooted through Rich's desk. She said, "What the hell kind of name is Rich Rice?"

Carl said, "Swear to god, he never talks."

Jen found a framed photo. It was Rich, three brothers, two gray parents, and six matching Christmas sweaters. "*Wow,*" she said, and though I hated Jen, hated her for dying her hair red and taking diet pills and flirting with our sociology professor, I laughed along. Matching sweaters, red and white. Rich and his brothers looked alike: perfect crop circles of brown hair, pale faces. Jen said, "I thought he was from Tulsa. Why would they need sweaters in the desert?"

Poor Jen had Tulsa confused with Tuscon. We mocked Jen relentlessly while Carl drew a map in the back of his Mandarin book. Laing laughed hardest. He hit her with Rich Rice's pillow. He found her ignorance charming.

I said, "At my Montessori school there was this wooden map of the US, and when the teacher wasn't looking we'd use Oklahoma as a gun."

Dolph said, "My uncle went to Oklahoma when he got divorced."

Jen wanted the crowd back. She lined up Rich's things on his bed: photo, calculator, seashell, shampoo. She said, "Who the hell is from Oklahoma anyway? What kind of person is from Oklahoma?"

We pawed the things. A museum of Oklahoma.

None of us had any idea.

by Rebecca Makkai

ILLUSTRATION BY DERRICK DENT

JEFF KEITH, LEAD SINGER OF TESLA, CONSIDERS YOUTH

There was that night in El Paso, or maybe Phoenix, where the singer for Cinderella started bleeding from his vocal chords. Every time he opened his mouth, like a fish, making this, like, yakking noise, it ended with red stains on the tile. It was some serious shit. It made you think about life, your body, how quick things could break down on the road. I was lucky. We were all so fucking lucky. We knew that. It wasn't like some riddle. Would you rather drive a septic truck around, or rock the fuck out of ten thousand paying customers? Shit.

But still, there were some nights when I thought about Oklahoma, being back in Idabel, even that one fucked up year in Broken Bow, and it wasn't any one thing, because those were some sorry-ass towns, and hot as all hell in summer, and flat and mean. You could walk along for miles and all you'd see is strip malls and the road throwing up heat, the graveyard with the names of all the young dudes who went to war and got killed. Those summers were like one long dead end.

So I don't understand, I can't tell you, why I still think about them, sweating through my raggedy-assed jeans, walking around looking for that one Indian kid Kevin to sell us his shitty weed, listening to the Doors and CCR and Steve fucking Miller, and wanting, for whole hours at a time, to be dead, or not seeing the difference anyway—until that one note finally arrives on the down-stroke and the singer's voice reaches up to nail it, and you do, too, all of you, singing, staring at each other, your dirty fucking hair and your pimples, and an actual breeze comes rolling in for the first time in a month, and with it the smell of rain, and you're like, Holy shit, dudes, this is cool. We're alive.

by Steve Almond

ILLUSTRATION BY BEE JOHNSON

NICOLAS CAGE'S AGENT

"I ate perhaps 1000 calories of Fig Newmans," said Nicolas Cage on Gmail chat to his agent who was currently in Ada, Oklahoma for her younger brother's wedding. "And 400 calories of Tate's cookies. In a time of severe depression."

"I ate a least 1000 calories of fries," said Nicolas Cage's agent.

"As people around me smoked marijuana," said Nicolas Cage.

"Waffle fries," said Nicolas Cage's agent.

"I also ate a bar panini," said Nicolas Cage.

"Did *you* smoke pot?" said Nicolas Cage's agent.

"No," said Nicolas Cage. "Well, sometimes."

"Bar Panini?" said Nicolas Cage's agent. "You mean, like a Luna Bar?"

"No," said Nicolas Cage. "A panini that I bought in a bar. There's a bar here … their thing is that they sell these paninis. I doubt they have paninis in Oklahoma."

Nicolas Cage's agent wasn't responding.

"Are you looking up 'panini' right now?" said Nicolas Cage. "It's, like, a sandwich or something. It's Italian I think. It's two things of flat bread with ham in between. Mine had ham, I think it's usually ham."

by Tao Lin

ILLUSTRATION BY DERRICK DENT

OF ALL PLACES

His mother said it was Oklahoma that was making him nuts, blaming the whole state when the only place he ever went was to work, which was 4.3 miles away, meaning that he actually inhabited a very small part of Oklahoma, certainly not enough of the state for it, collectively, to be blamed for making him nuts. Still, it was true that he had gone through his life, thirty-four years, not being nuts and then he had moved to Oklahoma and suddenly he was. He told his mother that maybe what had made him nuts was not Oklahoma but everything leading up to Oklahoma, his wife telling him that she might be in love with one of her students, though his wife taught eleventh-graders, and his mother calling every two seconds to see whether he'd left her yet. "Maybe it's you making me nuts," he told his mother, and she said, "Don't be silly."

"Of all places," his mother had said when he told her he was moving to Oklahoma, and he thought that the same could be said of the state she lived in, which was New Jersey. When he moved to New Mexico, where he met the wife who was now in love with a sixteen-year-old, everyone said, "Lucky you," people who had never even been to New Mexico, and when he'd moved to Minnesota, everyone said, "It's cold," as though he had no idea, but when he announced that he was moving to Oklahoma, people either said "Oklahoma?" like a question, or they began belting out the song from the musical, though most of them knew only the first word, which was "Oklahoma," singing it like it was a sentence on a rollercoaster, or a canoe gliding quietly down a river and then dropping straight over the edge of a waterfall.

by Lori Ostlund

PHOTO BY JUSTIN WHEELER

ENID, OKLAHOMA

An overhead fluorescent panel flickers and they awake in a gray concrete room. It's a perfect cube: the walls fifteen feet long, the ceiling fifteen feet high. It is empty except for a small rectangular cardboard box in one corner.

"It happened again," says Ralph, sitting up.

"You gotta be kidding me." Van rubs his forehead. He has an enormous shiner. "Hey—I got a shiner?"

Ralph shakes his head.

"That mean no?"

"It means I cannot believe it happened again." Ralph sighs. "Of course you have a shiner. It's only about the size of a cauliflower."

Van moans. "This the type of thing could only happen in Enid, Oklahoma."

"*Don't.*"

Ralph stands and approaches the wall.

"Why you bothering?" says Van. "You know there's no doors to this room."

Ralph palpates the surface, feeling for cracks. Van is right, of course. There are no doors.

Moaning again, Van staggers to his feet. He picks up the cardboard box, opens the lid, and flips it over. A thousand puzzle pieces spill to the ground. Every piece is slate gray on both sides, the exact same hue as the walls and the floor.

"Might as well get started. This one looks even harder than the last."

Ralph nods. They sit on the floor and start sorting through the pieces. But Ralph's heart isn't in it.

"Sorry," says Van. "What I said."

Ralph doesn't respond.

"About Enid."

"Enid has problems," says Ralph, looking up sharply. "I *know* that. But our problems are bigger."

They work on the puzzle for several minutes. Ralph, to his amazement, finds two pieces that fit together.

The light flickers. The room goes black. Ralph sighs. Van moans.

"We get outta this one," says Van, still feeling for the pieces, "I'll never say another word against Enid, Oklahoma."

"Yeah," says Ralph. "That's what you said last time."

by Nathaniel Rich

ILLUSTRATION BY SCOTT AUSTIN PRATHER

OKLAHOMA EXCLAMATION POINT

I met a famous person at a party. He emailed me a few days later, and I told him that a mutual acquaintance had been raving about him, had said he was the most honest and daring writer alive today, that seeing one of his plays was better than doing heroin. Usually I don't gush. It's embarrassing for everyone; it's sort of like showing up at a dinner party wearing a bunny costume and carrying a flaming dessert. But in this case, since it was second-hand and via email, I thought it was all right. The famous playwright (who was also preternaturally humble) emailed back: "Yeah, yeah," and asked if he could hitch a ride to Boston with me. I told him I'd be honored. "But you bring the music," I said. "Yesterday I was listening to the soundtrack to *Oklahoma!*, and you might not like that." He laughed and told me he'd bring some interpretations of *Oklahoma!* that were so far-out, I wouldn't even recognize or enjoy them.

He was right. I don't know in what universe these punk yodelers believed their music related to the beautiful songs of *Oklahoma!*, but after three minutes, I wanted out of my own car. Still, I didn't want to insult the famous playwright. Perhaps these people were his friends. Perhaps his next play was some kind of post-modern, amelodic reworking of *Oklahoma!*

"That's really interesting," I said, switching it off.

"You don't like it."

"It's not that. Some things are so good, you only need a little bit."

"Like caviar," he said.

"Like elk lasagna," I said. We passed a car with a vanity plate that said WHITHER.

"The best things always finish too quickly," he said.

by Alethea Black

ILLUSTRATION BY JEREMY LUTHER

TEXACO SIGN

Travelers say that all of Oklahoma is covered in a white fog. The only thing visible is a tall Texaco sign, and beneath it three enormous white plastic tiles with red letters that spell out EAT.

Maybe when you get there it's a plate of chicken, or maybe the sign keeps receding and receding and you never find out what there is to eat.

One report has come back about a coyote chasing a little white dog, but the sighting cannot be confirmed seeing that it may have been an illusion brought on by the fog.

by Jack Pendarvis

PHOTO BY ELIJAH ANDERSON

PAWN

That morning they'd awoke in South Dakota. Tonight they'd sleep somewhere in Texas. Tomorrow: Mexico. "You know," his father said, "you can call her from down there, too." But a promise was a promise, and they pulled up to a bar in a Panhandle town too small to have anything else.

Inside, the bartender poured him juice in a shot glass as a joke. His father laughed for him. Then started to ask questions in a language he didn't know. By the bathroom, a line of empty boots stood below a single wall-scrawled word: *pawn*. Beside the "p" a bag hung heavy with what looked, through stretched yellow plastic, like a bunch of shriveled hands. Beside the "n": a belt hanging like a snake nailed up by its head.

"You like that?" the bartender said. He said, "just a few hours ago," and "straight off the res," and "swapped it for a fifth." Laying it out, he traced the patterns, talked of its Indian beauty.

His father took out a twenty. "Throw in a call?" Pulled up the phone, set him on his lap.

"Oh thank God!" she said.

"Tell her," his father said, "we're in a bar."

"Frank?"

"I bought him a belt."

"Frank!" she shouted.

"Choctaw."

"I swear if you don't tell me where —"

"Oklahoma," the boy said.

In the silence after the bar phone slammed down, he could still hear his mother's breath about to turn into a word.

At the door, his father stopped him, crouched. The belt was so long it wrapped three times around his waist, the palm-sized buckle pressing at his belly.

Outside, there was a man leaning against the car. Brownfaced, blackeyed, a bottle in his hands. He saw them, straightened. "You think that's yours?" he said.

by Josh Weil

PHOTO BY LEROY COOP

QUAPAW, OK, 5/11

Stand in the sun in a parking lot as if to make an antique photo. Daily the sun shines your shadow, your negative, onto the asphalt. Where it makes no impression. Stand atop this pave for a year and you'd make no impression. *Oklahoma is not sensitive.*

by Joshua Cohen

PHOTO BY LAZLOW JONES

PAPERCRANE

I was moving from the mess in Almagordo to Pine Bluff and needed someone to drive my second car, a coughing '90 Volvo. My wife and three children had flown on ahead. I told them that one of my students, a man named Walt, was driving with me, but that was a lie. Walt wasn't driving —Papercrane was. Papercrane was our twenty-four-year-old neighbor who was now pregnant with a child I had been told was mine. I had my doubts about that fact but the truth is those doubts weren't very strong.

Just past Broken Arrow the sun had almost set. We were flanked by fields so alive with prairie dogs that I wished my children had been with me to see. We were otherwise alone on Highway 165 when behind me, in a flash, the Volvo jerked onto the shoulder and stopped. I'd been suspect of circumstance here, Papercrane so swollen with child and all, and now, my hands shaking, I felt the worst of my fears had been realized. I executed a slippery crossing of the grass median and turned back.

The Volvo's front windshield was shattered, a hole the size of a skillet punched in above the speedometer. The driver's door was open and from it I head Papercrane say "My God!" again and again and again. Shards of glass glimmered across her sweater. Blood trickled down her forehead. In the passenger seat a shivering prairie dog bled onto the map of southeastern Oklahoma and in her hands Papercrane held the intruding agent: a huge white owl.

"He just... boom!" she said. "What the fuck! And he had that!"

"You OK?" I said.

Then the bird lunged out of her hands and onto the heaving prey beside it. He turned. The face of that white beast scared me and I'm ashamed to say it now, but in a rush I kicked the door shut.

"Hey!" Papercrane said, and a strange sound began to emerge: it was the owl fluttering violently from within. There was no exit, though, not until Papercrane opened the door. But Papercrane didn't open the door. She wasn't even yelling any more. I didn't know what she was doing, because I was backing into a cornfield, afraid of the life enclosed therein. It was only the sound of something trapped, something now trying to escape, that echoed out there, dissipating into the darkening landscape around me.

by Nic Brown

ILLUSTRATION BY AUDREY BARCUS

SHARKS

It was six a.m. when the boys came to tell me that my coffin was ready. Up on deck, the sun was brutal, and Tio lunged toward me with sunblock. He was afraid I'd be too pink to look dead.

"For Christ's sake," I said, dodging his great coconut-scented hands. "Can't one of the girls do this?"

Tio ignored me. We'd first met while I was propping up the oil sector in Costa Rica, before I got kicked out for trying to open the machine gun factory. Tio did not take shit, especially from me. I would never have been a good swindler face-to-face; I couldn't have traveled around gaining the trust of wealthy widows. I emit an aura of disingenuousness even on those rare occasions when I'm feeling genuine. The wife I briefly had in Tulsa—Olivia: a very nice girl, though ultimately our ambitions differed—always told me I had no personal charisma. What I do have is ruthless intelligence and a spirited disrespect for the rule of law. This can get you pretty far in America—but, as I eventually found, only so far.

"It's going to be too short." Tio eyed the coffin, which still looked mostly like the pool table it recently had been.

Now the SEC is after me for something like $224 million. They've been chasing me around the coast of Antigua for years. Being driven into the sea isn't so bad if your boat has a sauna and discotheque; let nobody say I complain. And the night sea is beautiful—so much like basalt you half-believe you could walk on it if nobody was watching. But then, also, there's the corrosive salt, the interminable memories, your spinal fluid heaving always with the sea. Until, finally, I had an idea.

Rosario appeared. "So," she began powdering my face, pressing bruises under my eyes. "Whatcha gonna do when you're dead?"

"Read my obituaries." Shallow, obviously, but irresistible: I knew they'd been pre-written years ago, as is customary for celebrities. I wondered what Olivia would think when she read them.

"Of course." Rosario was painting lurid colors over my deadness—rouges to resurrect my lips, blushes to give my cheek a girlish, living tint. Once deemed sufficiently ghoulish, I climbed into the coffin.

"Squish down, boss," said Tio.

I squished, the sawdust curdling in my throat. The waves sounded violent against the hull. I hadn't told Rosario what I really wanted to do most, because it was defeatist. I wanted get off the boat. Shamefully, I did. I wanted a gleaming summer night. I wanted a city full of strangers.

Rosario bent over and gave me a rose for decoration, a rosary for irony. The sun was making me feel oddly vulnerable. "I can't keep my eyes open."

"Don't," said Tio cheerfully. "You're dead. Okay. Ready?"

I thought of land. I thought of tropical bugs like floating gemstones in the air.

"Rosario, no," said Tio. "Look sad. Like, frown. Boss? Hello?"

"Just getting into character." There was respectful quiet, and I could feel how sorrowful and rudderless they'd be without me. Maybe this was how Olivia had felt. Maybe I would ask her.

"Fine." I shut my eyes. "Go."

I thought of land, but all I saw was ocean. I saw green-gray eels, pulsing pink starfish.

I blinked and saw wood carved groupers. I clenched my eyes tighter and saw the shifting shadows of whales, and when the camera flashed I saw the luminescent bulbs of jellyfish. They glowed like planets, like the shore of a country where the future was happening without me.

by Jennifer DuBois

PHOTO BY ROSE RICHARDS

EXULTEMUS

I'd found my vocation.

"Your *what*?" said Beatrice.

"Hold still," said Mom, hemming Beatrice's costume.

"The Clares," I explained.

"Like Sister Michael of the holy dunce cap?" said Bea. We went to parochial school when we weren't on the road.

"You're *Bea*'s sister," said Pop.

I didn't say any more. I was expected to remain in song-and-dance with my family.

Next year Mom and Pop lucked into *Star and Garter*, a long run. Bea and I went back to school.

One afternoon I turned up at Miss de Mille's. OK she said. She yelled all the time. Flagellation had nothing on her. When she signed on as choreographer for a new show, *Away We Go*, she took us girls along. Rehearsals were hell. Mr. M was the devil made flesh, Mr. R and Mr. H quiet as martyrs.

Songs like hymns, ballets light as the Virgin's breath, costumes soft as swaddling.

Out-of-town try-outs? A mess! Numbers got pulled, dances rearranged, the show's name changed. I figured we'd close the first week in New York.

Opening night every damned one of us did our best. The audience clapped. Clapping is insufficient. Then came the production number. We made a wedge, Curley its point. We waved forward, singing. Backward, singing. Forward… The letters, one at a time, each louder than the one before, spelled a place I'll never see. But, calling its name, I experienced… ecstasy. The audience likewise. Kept us on Broadway five years.

During 2,212 performances did I fail to serve Mr. Rodgers and Mr. Hammerstein? No. I fulfilled my contract and cleared a nice bundle for my grateful family. After my novitiate I took vows. Left the stage behind.

But hollering *Oklahoma!* 2,212 times—that's praising the Lord, and don't let anybody tell you different.

by Edith Pearlman

ILLUSTRATION BY VINCENT NAPPI

THE REVERSE HIJACK

"Get the fuck in the truck!"

"You kidding me, old man?"

"If I were kidding would this fucking Glock be pointed at your dome? Get the fuck in the truck!"

Kevin Durant cradled the four basketballs under his massive wingspan and obediently stepped up onto the back of a twenty-six foot U-Haul.

"Got you, too, huh Kev?" came a baritone voice.

"Sure did, Perk."

"Westbrook and Harden are under the tarp playing dominoes sharing a turkey sub."

"Where we headin'? Back to Seattle?"

"Nah. Too obvious. That's the first place David Stern would look. I think I heard the old dude with the gun and the temper mention something about Santa Fe."

"So we'll be the Santa Fe Thunder?"

"He wants us to pitch him team nicknames on the way. There's an intercom on the wall over there."

"This could be really fun," said GM Sam Presti as he folded towels into thirds. "I love the marketing side of basketball."

"How about the Santa Fe Nets?" said a hopeful Nazr Mohammed, seated in a tiny folding chair on Serge Ibaka's lap.

"There's already a New Jersey Nets," proclaimed Presti.

"Yeah, but when they move to Brooklyn in 2012, I heard they'll be changing their name. So we'll only be sharing it for a season."

"How about the Santa Fe Westbrooks?" came a voice from under the tarp.

"A little too on-the-nose. But press the intercom and pitch it," blurted coach Scottie Brooks, stepping out of the shadows. "You never know."

"Dirk, what the hell are you doing here!? You're not even on our team!"

"Thabo Sefolosha called me up and asked if I'd help you guys move. Said there was some free pizza in it."

"Must've been Dwight Howard pulling another prank."

Then the old man with the Glock reappeared, fired several warning shots through the roof of the U-Haul and said Mapquest had fucked up the directions and he was now moving the team to Little Rock, Arkansas where they'd be nicknamed the Slammers.

by Brian Frazer

ILLUSTRATION BY JEFFERY ALLAN LOVE

BLACK WOUND

"We cannot stay another year; we want to go now, before another year has passed, we may all be dead, and there will be none of us left to travel north."

—Chief Morning Star of the Cheyenne
Oklahoma, 1877

We all came from the wound. Dry red dirt on the soles of their feet, the families of the fighting Cheyenne escaped an Oklahoma prison camp in darkness. Big land, Oklahoma, and fertile like the arms of a lover. But in the dawn of that age a tide of destiny was made manifest and rode west like a beast of prey, and none were safe and none secure and all were eaten and devoured and scattered. "North, we must go north," said Dull Knife, "and if we die, we die north. Not here, where we die like dogs." And so Dull Knife's band gathered their small number and fled under cover of night, fighting at the rearguard with pursuant Cavalry, advancing with the vanguard back to the home country. Their teeth dry and white, they moved fast, and water pulled at their wind-torn eyes and night went to day and day fell again to night. Farther north and farther west they met their end in an unholy place made desolate with body and one and blood.

Northward, flurries of snow placed white ledges on the limbs of trees and as the band progressed the sky turned densely opaque until land and sky were one and the edges of the world had smoothed into a blanket under which their dreams and desires slept like animals of a forgotten country, like bears under the dark pull of den and body and breath.

Split and split again, the band was small, and tracked and cornered, captured. Imprisoned a second time, the shadow of a raven's wing fell on the heads of women and men. Led by Big Bear, the number only 30, the people undestroyed, they stood together and pronounced what must not be pronounced. Surrounded by sentinels at Fort Robinson, locked in, starved, the men were separated from the women, and the women, on occasion allowed to go to them. Here the women spoke fiercely to their husbands, "Take your stand. Die fighting. We cannot go back. We cannot go forward. Die with dignity. We are with you. We love you forever." And Big Bear answered, "Yes. I have lived enough. I am ready." And together, the men said, "If our women are willing to die with us, who is there to say no? If we are to do the deeds of men, bring us our guns." And the women smiled and in their hearts they sang the dying song, and aloud they said, "We have hidden your weapons in the folds of our clothing," and under concealment of night and sky the women brought forth pieces of the weapons, and the men assembled the weapons and stored them under a floorboard for the appointed time.

The men killed the sentinels first, and took their guns. Then the Cheyenne fled to the nearest gully, women and men and children, and braced themselves. The blue soldiers came on with vengeance in their eyes and rage in the marbled pillars of their necks, hordes of men alive in the predawn dark.

The Cheyenne warriors raised their guns until the bullets were gone.

Then they bared their chests to the enemy.

The women stood and held their children up toward the oncoming light.

They died together in that place.

Black wound against the winter white.

by Shann Ray

ILLUSTRATION BY LESLIE HERMAN

OKLAHOMAN MIDRASH

In the beginning there was dust: an ocean of it. The dust lacked form, lacked life. This grieved God, who then cried amidst the dust until there was mud below, and mud above: a wobbling firmament of mud. God brooded over that mud, breathed over it, and then mud became man.

Some time passed. Men-from-mud began to misbehave. Egregiously. Feeling the pain of his hands' work, God grieved. It was a larger grief than that first one, the one that poured form into dust. This grief was shaped by the recollection of specific evils, harm that his creation had worked upon each other and the terrible knowledge that it would continue. This grief was not of the nutritive sort. And God knew it. God cried for his creation that would not be able to withstand his sorrow. The lives that those lives might have engendered, if given more time—he lamented for them, too. He cried because sorrow was so often a lop-sided engagement: people rarely grieve together for the same reasons at the same time and with the exact same measure of sorrow. Sorrow is unique, and therefore, misunderstood.

Which is why God had sent a series of preemptive rescues: flotation device experts offering in-home inspections at absolutely no charge to all who said *yes.* Samples large and small: butterfly wings, life jackets, neon colored foam noodles. Then came the flotilla of canoes, life rafts, inflatable porpoises, and plastic crocodiles—also free.

But it had been hotter than blazes, the heat searing the color out of grass, wood, air. The heat turned streets to rivers of tar. It had been so hot, that no one could take seriously these gifts of air corralled in tensile materials approved for water sports and nautical adventures everywhere. These offerings seemed like jokes in poor taste: especially the admonition *repent!* How insulting—the implication that a sudden climactic change might have anything, anything at all do to with them. This is what provoked homeowners and renters young and old to draw their blinds, bolt their doors, roll plugs of cotton into their ears.

At the sound of such unified refusal, such willed rejection, God's sorrow increased exponentially. Neither casements of sky nor wellsprings of deep could contain it. From above and below water rose and fell. God, as he had in the beginning, hovered and brooded over the dark and roiling waters. Days passed. Near Day 27 God brooded his way toward regret. The floodwaters receded. On Day 33 God remembered something—another incidence of human harm done purely for recreational purposes, and then he felt sorrow. The floodwaters rose. That's how Godly sorrow works: it ebbs and flows. It's like the breath of the breath of life. There. And then, at times, less there. It's enough to fool the uninitiated.

Which is the reason for the rainbow: a reminder for those who would doubt the potency of sorrow. A promise that should God become grieved in the heart at some later date, he'd not resort to tears. Other reminders: in low places, flats and sinks, places like Uzbekistan or, say, Oklahoma, God's tears dried to salt. Thirst. Dust. From time to time people dig in such places and find evidence of life before the big sorrow: elongated fishes and fronds of plants stretched by the pressure of so much water. They hold these items in their hands, speak of them with wonder and awe.

by Gina Ochsner

PHOTO BY SHANE BROWN

TEARS

Here, all the tears of the trail of tears fell, and now look.

by Padgett Powell

ILLUSTRATION BY MARIE PROVENCE

THE MIGRATION

Men had taken back up the much-sung practice of stepping out for smokes and never returning home, and it seemed all these men were winding up in Oklahoma. Deadbeats from the Mississippi Delta, the Carolinas, even the bustling sarcastic Eastern cities, and some from the West, unraveling the sorry destinies they'd manifested. These men had wanton meanness to vent and many were out of cash. They had, in the only matter that matters, failed. The latest trouble was someone had stolen a hulking ancient piano from Second Baptist. The empty space where the instrument had sat looked like a parcel of the moon and the Sheriff couldn't get it out of his mind. Before all the boarding houses had filled he always had a suspect in mind for any crime, and then he could attempt to prove the suspect innocent and often he was successful and often happily so. He didn't know any of these first-time drifters from the Mayor of Pittsburgh. He didn't know what they would or wouldn't conceive, what they could or couldn't carry out.

The Sheriff had a pair of deputies, junior and senior, though the titles didn't indicate differing prowess or promotion due to merit. Gil had been in the job a year longer was all. Gil's talent was for brewing perfect coffee and Tommy could twist up balloon animals when field trips stopped by the station. They could both grapple tolerably well. The Sheriff and his deputies hadn't solved a case in months and when the Sheriff brought in the girl he told folks it was to show up his deputies, to light a fire under them. The girl was said to be psychic but the word used these days was "clairvoyant". The Sheriff took Tommy's desk and told him to sit in the empty receptionist's station. The Sheriff was pulling a stunt, whatever the reason, by bringing in the girl. Deep down he had always believed in curses and gods and ghosts. The girl had still long fingers and hair that looked gray in most light and that she usually kept hung down her front and often clung to with two hands like someone clinging to a rope. The girl's own father had run off. She was said to have Indian blood but she was probably as white as Garth Brooks. She didn't sit at Tommy's desk but instead went onto the back patio and shimmied the helium tank into the autumn sun and filled balloon after balloon and watched them float into the sky. The Sheriff watched her for what felt like most of the day but was about fifteen minutes. He went out and stood near her with a quizzical yet open expression on his face.

She said, "When a balloon disappears, I hear the piano."

by John Brandon

PHOTO BY LOGAN PIERSEN

YELLOW WEATHER

Shaped like a hatchet or a gun or a pot, flat as a pan or a block or a beach but dry, cracked, cruel, buffeted by wind and yellowing weather, this state is in a state of danger only Mother and Father, sleepless, see until the knock at the door wakes my sisters and me, and the motel manager gravely informs us of what the stillness portends: tornado. He has come to offer us shelter because there are children— we three are children—the only children at the U-Right Motel on this night in May. "Follow me," he says, and we do, Mother, Father, my sisters and me. Barefoot in blankets, we children follow the bobbing light to the shelter and down the stairs— oldest first, which means I'm last and most afraid, in tears. Mother is saying, It's ok, it's ok, it's ok, we're safe, when the hatch is yet open and the wind is a whine, and my sister, the oldest, the worst, that brat, says she's forgotten her jewelry, she needs her jewelry. Her jewelry? Mother asks. Glass beads, brass bracelets, cheap metals that go green are my oldest sister's valuables, yet Mother goes back even as the wind rubbles doors, tumbles baskets and empty barrels. Oklahoma is rolling over us and over our Mother who is where? She has abandoned us. Later, she will tell us how she saved herself, curled away from the windows and waited it out while I wailed in the shelter, inconsolable. The jewels were found, but for as long as the day, I wouldn't speak to my mother; I wished she were dead.

by Christine Schutt

ILLUSTRATION BY JEREMY LUTHER

THE VIOLINIST

They move with inhuman speed, the commuters, and it took me some time to get used to this. I myself am not a fast man.

"That's because you're eighty-three," my brother-in-law Joachim says on the phone. I've yet to explain to his satisfaction why I sold my farm and moved to the city. His sister, my wife, has been dead for two years.

"Eighty-two," I say. He knows how old I am. We've known one another since we were both seventeen. "And I don't think I was ever fast."

I lived all my life on a farm and by the time I was old enough to have a farm of my own, small-scale farming had become mostly a matter of watching. You watch the robots move over the fields. You tinker with their settings sometimes but they're well-made, they adjust themselves mostly, they don't need you for much. You play your violin in the field just to keep yourself occupied. In the distance the airships rise with the speed of fireflies, but they're faster up close: now when I play my violin at the airship terminal they ascend so quickly that it's as if they're falling upward, gravity reversed.

I play Beethoven and watch the commuters, blank-faced between their earbuds, rushing to their gates. They glance at me sometimes, toss coins in my violin case. I thank them, try to make eye contact. I watch their ships carry them up into the early morning, to jobs in Los Angeles, Boston, New York. I think of their souls moving fast through the morning sky.

When my wife died I kept up the farm for another year and then thought, to hell with it. I felt that without her I might disappear into thin air, out there by myself. Just me and the dog and the farm robots, day after day. All that empty space. At night I sat on the porch with my dog, avoiding the silent house. Playing the game kids play, where you squint at the moon and half-convince yourself that you can see the brighter spots of the colonies on its surface. Distant over the fields, the lights of the city, and I realized I'd been longing for those lights all my life.

"I'll take you with me," I said to my dog, Odie, who doesn't know he was named after a much dumber dog from a comic strip my grandparents read, and he wagged his tail.

"Oklahoma City," Joachim said, when I called him that night. "John, brother, you'll get swallowed alive there."

But I wasn't. I've been thinking about time and motion lately, about being a still point in the ceaseless rush. I walk my dog through these streets and play my violin in the airship terminal, happy in a way I can't explain, and I don't need the coins tossed into the case but it's a comfort in this seething crowd to be seen.

by Emily St. John Mandel

ILLUSTRATION BY MATT GOAD

AUTHORS

CHANDLER BURR, the *New York Times* perfume critic from 2006-2010, is the director and curator of the Center of Olfactory Art at the Museum of Arts and Design in New York City. His debut novel, *You or Someone Like You*, was published in 2009.

JOHN CROWLEY is the author of a dozen novels, including *Little, Big* and *The Aegypt Cycle*. He lives in northwestern Massachusetts and teaches creative writing at Yale.

CAROLYN PARKHURST is the author of the novels *The Dogs of Babel*, *Lost and Found*, and *The Nobodies Album*. She has published fiction in the *North American Review*, the *Minnesota Review*, *Hawai'i Review*, and *Crescent Review*. She received a B.A. from Wesleyan University and an M.F.A. in creative writing from American University. She lives in Washington, D.C., with her husband and two children.

ADAM LANGER is the author of a memoir and four novels including *Crossing California* and *The Thieves of Manhattan*. He divides his time between Bloomington, Indiana, and New York City where he is at work on a few new novels.

ALETHEA BLACK'S debut collection of short stories, *I Knew You'd Be Lovely*, was a Barnes & Noble Discover Great New Writers pick. Black's work has won the Arts & Letters Prize, has been cited as distinguished in *The Best American Short Stories*, and has been read at venues around the country.

GINA OCHSNER lives in Keizer, Oregon and divides her time between writing and teaching with the Seattle Pacific Low-Residency MFA program. Ochsner has been awarded a John L. Simon Guggenheim grant and a grant from the National Endowment of Arts. Her stories have appeared in the *New Yorker*, *Tin House*, *Glimmer Train*, and *Kenyon Review*. She is the author of the short story collection *The Necessary Grace to Fall*, which received the Flannery O'Connor Award for Short Fiction and the story collection *People I Wanted to Be*. Both books received the Oregon Book Award. Her novel entitled *The Russian Dreambook of Colour and Flight* was published in 2009.

BROCK CLARKE is the author of five books, most recently *Exley* (which was named a *Kirkus* book of the year) and *An Arsonist's Guide to Writers' Homes in New England* (which was a national bestseller and has appeared in a dozen foreign editions). His stories and essays have appeared in the *Virginia Quarterly Review, One Story, The Believer, Georgia Review, Southern Review, The New York Times*, and *Ninth Letter* and have appeared in the annual *Pushcart Prize* and *New Stories from the South* anthologies and on NPR's Selected Shorts. He is the *Boston Globe*'s "By the Book" columnist, and teaches creative writing at Bowdoin College.

MARY JO BANG is the author of six volumes of poetry, most recently, *The Bride of E*, and *Elegy*, which received the National Book Critics Circle Award. She lives in St. Louis and teaches at Washington University.

SHANN RAY holds a PhD in psychology from the University of Alberta. His work has appeared in *McSweeney's*, *Narrative Magazine*, *Story Quarterly*, and other publications. He played college basketball at Montana State University and Pepperdine University and played professional basketball in Germany. He lives with his wife and three daughters in Spokane, Washington, where he teaches leadership and forgiveness studies at Gonzaga University.

BRIAN FRAZER is a former stand-up comic who has also written for a variety of television shows, including *Mad TV*, *The Tom Green Show,* and *Blind Date*, where he met his wife, Nancy, when they were both thought-bubble writers. He now writes regularly for *Esquire* and *ESPN Magazine* and has a monthly column for *Los Angeles Magazine*. Brian has also written for *Vanity Fair*, *Premiere,* and *Maxim*. He is the author of the book *Hyper-Chondriac: A Memoir.*

WAYNE KOESTENBAUM has published five books of poetry, one novel, and six books of nonfiction. A graduate of Harvard and Princeton, he is a distinguished professor of English at the CUNY Graduate Center and a visiting professor in the painting department of the Yale School of Art.

JACK PENDARVIS is the author of one novel and two collections of short stories. He teaches in the MFA program at Ole Miss and is a columnist for *Oxford American* and *The Believer*. His work has appeared in many other publications, including *McSweeney's*, and *The New York Times*.

MATT BONDURANT'S latest novel is *The Night Swimmer*. His second novel, *The Wettest County in the World*, was a *New York Times* Editor's Pick and one of *San Francisco Chronicle's* Best 50 Books of the Year. His first novel, *The*

Third Translation, was an international bestseller, translated into 14 languages worldwide. A former John Gardner Fellow in Fiction at Bread Loaf, Kingsbury Fellow at Florida State, and Walter E. Dakin Fellow at Sewanee, he currently lives in Texas.

DEBORAH WILLIS was born and raised in Calgary, Alberta, Canada. Her fiction has appeared in *Grain*, *Event*, *Prism International*, and *The Walrus*. Her first book, *Vanishing and Other Stories*, was named one of the *Toronto Globe and Mail's* Best Books of 2009, and was nominated for the BC Book Prize and the Governor General's Award. She has worked as a horseback riding instructor and a reporter, and currently works as a bookseller in Victoria, British Columbia.

NATHANIEL RICH is the author of *The Mayor's Tongue*. His second novel is forthcoming from Farrar, Straus & Giroux.

TAO LIN is the author of six books of fiction/poetry. He has a B.A. in Journalism from New York University and lives in Brooklyn, New York. His second novel, *Richard Yates,* was published in 2010 by Melville House.

STEVE ALMOND is the author of the story collections *God Bless America,* winner of the 2012 Paterson Fiction Prize, *The Evil B.B. Chow,* and *My Life in Heavy Metal;* the novel *Which Brings Me to You* (with Julianna Baggott); and the nonfiction books *Rock and Roll Will Save Your Life,(Not That You Asked),* and *Candyfreak.* His stories have appeared in *Playboy, Zoetrope, Ploughshares,* and *Ecotone,* among other magazines, and have been reprinted in *Best American Short Stories* and *The Pushcart Prize.*

REBECCA MAKKAI is a Chicago-based writer whose first novel, *The Borrower,* has garnered rave reviews in *O Magazine*, *BookPage*, and *Booklist* among others. Her short fiction will appear in *The Best American Short Stories* this fall for the fourth consecutive year, and appears regularly in journals like *Tin House*, P*loughshares*, *New England Review* and *Shenandoah*.

BEN GREENMAN is an editor at *The New Yorker* and author of several acclaimed books of fiction, including *Superbad*, *Superworse*, and *A Circle is a Balloon and Compass Both: Stories About Human Love*. His fiction, essays, and journalism have appeared in numerous publications, including *The New York Times*, *Washington Post, Paris Review*, *Zoetrope: All Story*, *McSweeney's*, and *Opium* and he has been widely anthologized.

LORI OSTLUND'S first collection of stories, *The Bigness of the World*, received the 2008 Flannery O'Connor Award for Short Fiction, the California Book Award for First Fiction, and the Edmund White Debut Fiction Award, was a Lambda finalist, and a 2009 Story Prize Notable Book. Stories from the collection have appeared in the *Best American Short Stories, The PEN/O. Henry Prize Stories*, *Kenyon Review*, *New England Review*, *Prairie Schooner,* and *Georgia Review*, among other publications. She was the recipient of a Rona Jaffe Foundation Writers' Award and a fellowship to the Bread Loaf Writers' Conference. She lives in San Francisco but is currently the Kenan Visiting Writer at UNC-Chapel Hill.

ALAN HEATHCOCK'S fiction has been published in many of America's top magazines and journals, including *Zoetrope: All Story*, *Kenyon Review*, *VQR*, *Five Chapters*, *Storyville*, and *The Harvard Review*. His stories have won the National Magazine Award for fiction, and have been selected for inclusion in *The Best American Mystery Stories* anthology. *VOLT*, a collection of stories published by Graywolf Press, received starred reviews from *Library Journal* and *Publishers Weekly*, a *New York Times* Editors' Choice, featured as one of three notable debuts to watch on *The Huffington Post*, selected as a Barnes & Noble Best Book of the Month, as well as for inclusion in the Barnes & Noble Discover Great New Writers series. Heathcock has been awarded fellowships from the Sewanee Writers' Conference and Bread Loaf Writers' Conference, and is currently a Literature Fellow for the state of Idaho. A native of Chicago, he teaches fiction writing at Boise State University.

AIMEE BENDER is the author of four books: *The Girl in the Flammable Skirt* (1998) which was a *New York Times* Notable Book, *An Invisible Sign of My Own* (2000) which was an *Los Angeles Times* pick of the year, *Willful Creatures* (2005) which was nominated by *The Believer* as one of the best books of the year, and *The Particular Sadness of Lemon Cake (*2010), which recently won the SCIBA award for best fiction and an Alex Award.

EMILY ST. JOHN MANDEL was born on the west coast of British Columbia, Canada. She studied dance at The School of Toronto Dance Theatre and lived briefly in Montreal before relocating to New York. Her third novel, *The Lola Quartet,* was the #1 Indie Next pick for May 2012. Her previous novels are *Last Night in Montreal* (a June 2009 Indie Next pick and a finalist for ForeWord Magazine's 2009 Book of the Year) and *The Singer's Gun* (winner of an Indie Bookseller's Choice Award, #1 Indie Next pick for May 2010, long-listed for both The Morning News' 2011 Tournament of Books and the 2011 Spinetingler Awards.)

CRAIG MORGAN TEICHER is the author of *Brenda Is in the Room and Other Poems,* awarded the 2007 Colorado Prize for Poetry. He also wrote *Cradle*

Book (2010), a collection of fiction and fables. Teicher serves as vice president of the National Book Critics Circle. He is senior web editor and poetry reviews editor of *Publishers Weekly* and teaches at The New School and Columbia University. Craig lives in Brooklyn with his wife and son.

CHRISTINE SCHUTT is the author of a short story collections *Nightwork* and *A Night, A Day, Another Night, Summer.* The former was chosen by poet John Ashbery as the best book of 1996 for the *Times Literary Supplement*. Her first novel *Florida* was a National Book Award finalist for fiction in 2004. Her second novel *All Souls* was a Pulitzer Prize for fiction finalist in 2009. Her new novel *Prosperous Friends* is out now from Grove Press.

NIC BROWN is the author of the novel *Doubles* and the story collection *Floodmarkers*, which was selected as an Editor's Choice by *The New York Times* Book Review. His writing has appeared in *The New York Times*, *Garden & Gun*, and *Harvard Review*, among many other publications. He is currently the John and Renee Grisham Writer in Residence at the University of Mississippi.

JENNIFER DUBOIS was born in Northampton, Massachusetts in 1983. She earned a B.A. in political science and philosophy from Tufts University and an M.F.A. in fiction from the Iowa Writers' Workshop, where she was a Teaching-Writing Fellow. After completing a Stegner Fellowship in fiction, Jennifer served as the Nancy Packer Lecturer in Continuing Studies at Stanford University. Her writing has appeared or is forthcoming in *Playboy, The Wall Street Journal, Esquire* and *Byliner's* "New Voices" collection, *Missouri Review*, *Kenyon Review*, *Florida Review*, *Northwest Review*, *Narrative*, *ZYZZYVA*, *FiveChapters* and elsewhere. Her short story "Wolf" was named a Notable Story in Best American Short Stories 2012, and the first chapter of *A Partial History of Lost Causes* was selected as a Top Five Story of 2011-2012 by *Narrative*. Jennifer was recently honored by the National Book Foundation's 5 Under 35 program. *A Partial History of Lost Causes* is her first novel.

LAUREN GROFF is the author of *The Monsters of Templeton*, which was a *New York Times* and *Booksense* bestseller, shortlisted for the Orange Prize for New Writers, and translated into over a dozen languages. Her second book, *Delicate Edible Birds*, is a collection of stories, some of which have *appeared in The Atlantic Monthly, One Story, Ploughshares, Glimmer Train*, T*he Best New American Voices*, and *The Best American Short Stories* 2007 and 2010. She has won a Pushcart Prize and a PEN/O.Henry Prize, has published fiction in the *New Yorker,* and was awarded the Axton Fellowship in Fiction. Her second novel, *Arcadia*, will be published this spring. Richard Russo said of the novel,

"*Arcadia* is one of the most moving and satisfying novels I've read in a long time." She lives in Gainesville, Florida, with her husband and two sons.

JOSH WEIL was born in the Appalachian Mountains of rural Virginia to which he returned to write the novellas in his first book, *The New Valley*. A *New York Times* Editors Choice, *The New Valley* won the Sue Kaufman Prize for First Fiction from The American Academy of Arts and Letters; the New Writers Award from the GLCA; a "5 Under 35" Award from the National Book Foundation; and was shortlisted for the Library of Virginia's literary award in fiction. Weil's other fiction has appeared in such publications as *Granta, One Story* and *Agni*, and he has written non-fiction for *The New York Times*, *Oxford American*, and *Poets & Writers*. The recipient of fellowships and awards from the Fulbright Foundation, the Dana Foundation, the Bread Loaf and Sewanee Writers' Conferences, the James Merrill House, Gilman School, Virginia Center for the Creative Arts, and the MacDowell Colony, he has taught at Bowling Green State University as the Distinguished Visiting Writer and as the Grisham Writer-in-Residence at the University of Mississippi. These days he lives in the mountains of northern California, where he is finishing a novel — *The Great Glass Sea*, forthcoming from Gove/Atlantic in late 2013.

EDITH PEARLMAN received the 2011 PEN/Malamud award for excellence in short fiction, honoring her four collections of stories: *Vaquita*, *Love Among the Greats*, *How To Fall*, and *Binocular Vision*. *Binocular Vision,* published by Lookout Books, received several 2011 awards: from the National Book Critics Circle, the Boston Authors' Club, and the University of Hartford (the Edward Lewis Wallant prize). It was a finalist for other prizes: the National Book Award in fiction, the Story Prize, and the *Los Angeles Times'* award in fiction. Pearlman's work has appeared in *Best American Short Stories* (4 times), *O. Henry Prize* stories (3 times), *Pushcart Prize Stories* (twice), and *Best Stories from the South* and *Best Non-Required Reading* (once each).

ALEXANDER YATES' first novel, *Moondogs*, was published in 2011 by Doubleday. His stories have appeared or are forthcoming in *Salon*, *Kenyon Review,* and *American Fiction.*

ANNA SOLOMON'S first novel, *The Little Bride*, was published by Riverhead. Her stories and essays have appeared in *The New York Times Magazine, One Story, Harvard Review, Georgia Review, Missouri Review,* and elsewhere, and have twice been awarded the Pushcart Prize. Anna lives in Providence, Rhode Island, with her husband and daughter.

JESS ROW is the author of two collections of stories, *The Train to Lo Wu* and *Nobody Ever Gets Lost*, which *Library Journal* recently described as "one of the six best works of fiction about September 11th." His work has appeared in *The Atlantic, Tin House, Granta, Conjunctions*, and three times in *The Best American Short Stories.* He teaches at the College of New Jersey and the Vermont College of Fine Arts.

PADGETT POWELL is the author of five novels, including *The Interrogative Mood* and *Edisto*, which was nominated for the National Book Award. His writing has appeared in *The New Yorker*, *Harper's*, *Little Star*, and *The Paris Review*, and he has received a Whiting Writers' Award and the Rome Fellowship in Literature from the American Academy of Arts and Letters. He lives in Gainesville, Florida, where he teaches writing at MFA@FLA, the writing program of the University of Florida.

LAURIE NOTARO'S latest book, *It Looked Different on the Model,* is probably still available at bookstores. Hopefully. Fingers crossed. She lives in Oregon where she is on anti-depressants, has a HappyLight, and moss grows inside of her car.

JOE MENO is a fiction writer and playwright who lives in Chicago. A winner of the Nelson Algren Literary Award, a Pushcart Prize, a Great Lakes Book Award, and a finalist for the Story Prize, he is the author of five novels, *The Great Perhaps, The Boy Detective Fails, Hairstyles of the Damned, How the Hula Girl Sings*, and *Tender as Hellfire.*

NANCY MAURO is the author of the novel *New World Monkeys*, named one of *Publishers Weekly's* Best Books of 2009 and a *USA Today* "New Voices" selection. Mauro has worked as a creative director and copywriter in both Canada and the U.S. and now lives in Brooklyn.

WILLIAM LYCHACK is the author of a novel, *The Wasp Eater,* and a collection of stories, *The Architect of Flowers*. His work has appeared in *The Best American Short Stories,* and on public radio's *This American Life.*

JONATHAN LETHEM is the author of seven novels. A recipient of the MacArthur Fellowship, Lethem has also published his stories and essays in *The New Yorker*, *Harper's*, *Rolling Stone*, *Esquire*, and *The New York Times*, among others.

RACHEL KUSHNER is the author of *Telex from Cuba*, which was a finalist for the National Book Award in Fiction in 2008, a finalist for the Dayton Literary Peace Prize, and winner of the California Book Award. Kushner's writing has appeared in *Artforum*, *Bookforum*, the *New York Times*, *Fence*,

Bomb, *The Believer*, *Cabinet,* and *Grand Street*. She is an editor of the journal *Soft Targets* and lives in Los Angeles.

JUSTIN TAYLOR is the author of *The Gospel of Anarchy,* a novel, and *Everything Here Is the Best Thing Ever,* a collection of short stories. He lives in Brooklyn, NY and online at *justindtaylor.net*

CAITLIN HORROCKS is author of the short story collection *This Is Not Your City* (Sarabande Books, 2011). Her fiction appears in *The New Yorker*, *The Best American Short Stories* 2011, *The Paris Review*, and elsewhere. She teaches at Grand Valley State University and lives in Grand Rapids, Michigan.

JOSHUA COHEN is the author of three novels. *Four New Messages*, a collection of novellas, was published by Graywolf Press in 2012.

STEPHEN DAU is originally from Western Pennsylvania and attended the University of Pittsburgh before working in post-war reconstruction in the Balkans and international philanthropy in Washington D.C. He subsequently studied creative writing at Johns Hopkins University and received an MFA from the Bennington Writing Seminars. In addition to his debut novel, *The Book of Jonas*, his work has appeared in *The Pittsburgh Post-Gazette, McSweeney's,* and MSNBC, among other places. He lives in Brussels.

TUPELO HASSMAN'S first novel, *girlchild*, was published this year by Farrar, Straus and Giroux. Her work has also appeared in *The Boston Globe, Paper Street Press, Portland Review Literary Journal, Tantalum, We Still Like, ZYZZYVA,* and by 100WordStory.org, FiveChapters.com, and Invisible City Audio Tours. Tupelo collected footage of *girlchild*'s book tour for a short documentary, *Hardbound: A Novel's Life on the Road*, which may or may not have been a terrible idea.

JOHN BRANDON was raised on the Gulf Coast of Florida. He spent the last two years at Ole Miss and this coming year will be teaching at Gilman School in Baltimore. He has written two novels, *Arkansas* and *Citrus County*, both from *McSweeney's*, the latter of which has recently been released in paperback. His shorter work has appeared in *GQ*, *The Oxford American*, *Subtropics*, *The New York Times Magazine*, *McSweeney's Quarterly Concern*, *The Believer*, *Mississippi Review*, *Tampa Review*, *Saw Palm*, *ESPN* the *Magazine*, *The Pinch*, and *Yalobusha Review*. Last season he wrote a blog on SEC football for GQ.com and this coming fall he will write about all of college football for Grantland.com.

ACKNOWLEDGMENTS

BY JEFF MARTIN

The realization of this project is due in large part to the work, advice, creativity and general enthusiasm provided by everyone at This Land Press. Special thanks to Vincent LoVoi, Michael Mason, Mark Brown, Courtney Campbell, Holly Wall, Natasha Ball, Abby Wendle, Sarah Geis, Sterlin Harjo, Matt Leach, Carlos Knight, David Duncan, Kathryn Parkman, Stuart Hetherington, Claire Edwards, and Cecilia Whitehurst. Taking this idea from concept to creation would have been nearly impossible without the art direction provided by Jeremy Luther. Lastly, my unending gratitude to the dozens of authors and artists that dared to imagine the place I call home, and in doing so, forever changed the way I see it.

www.ingramcontent.com/pod-product-compliance
Lightning Source LLC
Chambersburg PA
CBHW041642010726
47507CB00012B/433

9781480036291